Chaos Queen
The Lost Queen Duet

N.OWENS

Chaos Queen: The Lost Queen Duet

Copyright © 2023 by N.OWENS in USA.

All rights reserved.

Cover by: GetCovers

Dedication

This book is dedicated to all the women out there that need a
reminder that you are a queen. So, hold your head up high, straighten
that spine and give the middle finger to whoever tries to tell you
differently.

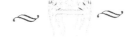

P.S. I recommed adding a "Fuck You" to any man who tries to tell you
you're not a queen

CONTENTS

"A powerful king should always rule with
a humble queen by his side.
But make no mistake that, yes while the king is powerful; in a
game of chess the queen is to be all powerful and feared."

-N.OWENS

PROLOGUE
FALSE QUEEN

"What do you mean, you can't find her? It's been three years, this is it, Frank. If she turns eighteen and I'm not there to claim her power, what do you think will happen? Hmmm."

Frank bows his head. Like he should in my presence. This is ridiculous. I've sent hundreds of my scouts to look for her and they keep coming back with no results. I know she isn't dead, sadly I can feel the dumb bitch's power still. I won't let an insignificant young girl attempt to take what is rightfully mine. The thrown and this crown should be mine by birthright, but no, this bitch had to be born with the stupid true queen mark.

I grab this useless being by the throat and pull him closer to me. "She turns 18 in less than a month. And I need her here. Send everyone, find her or else." I toss him to the floor. Turning away and to the empty room. "Find her or your neck is on the line."

"Yes, my queen. We may have a lead. I will send some men to look into it." I wave my hand to dismiss him.

Her power will be mine. Till then maybe mommy dearest will give me more information about transferring power.

I head down to the dungeon of my personal quarters. No one knows this area exists and it will stay that way until I get what I want. I can't have anyone knowing of my guests down here. Entering the room, I look around and spot my target.

Glading done the hallway, I pass the six cells that occupy this room. Sadly, only four hold someone because of one of my fathers dying in the attack, but I suppose it all worked out according to my plans. My mother hasn't had the strength to fight back since his death. I walk past my other so-called fathers as they look up and glare at me. Oh well, I have come to terms with knowing a queen can't always be loved.

I stop at the cage that I want and see my mother stand and put my younger brother Jasper behind her. Like I care for his power. Ha.

"Well, good evening, mother." I say with a sweet smile. "We are getting closer to her."

I hear her intake of breath and I smile wider. "Yes. Soon, I will truly be all that is left of the royal line. I will be the most powerful supernatural ever to walk this realm. All thanks to your precious little marked queen." I sneer.

My mother raises her chin, and I narrow my eyes at her.

"Margo. My once sweet Margo. Your sister may have lost the true future she was to have, but I assure you, she will be the true queen. Fate has shown me. You will fall and lose it all."

No! I lash out, my power striking her across the cheek, but she remains calm and still.

"Her power will be mine, mother, whether she gives it freely to me or I have to rip out her heart to get it. I have worked too hard for too long for some useless, naïve little girl who doesn't even know of this realm or her kind to take it away from me." I hiss at her. How dare she even think that? "I will make you watch as I drain her of her soul and magic. I promise you that, Queen Ava." I spit out.

I turn and storm out of the room. Azzie's power will be mine and I will kill anyone who gets in my way.

Tick Tock. The clock is ticking, little sister, and soon your time will be up.

ONE

AZZIE

My head is pounding as I stretch out my body. What the hell happened last night? Ugh, did I drink again? No. I remember being at school, Cas demanding I talk to him in art, and then Gym. Ugh. The entire school seeing my scars. Beasty. *Holy shit!* I saw a real-life dragon, and man was it better than reading about ones in books. Then finding out that when someone shifts back from a shifted beast form, they are naked.

Shit. I totally saw Max's junk. But it was such nice junk. Okay, okay, what else? *Think, think Azzie.*

Bella and Cas arguing. Bella saying that they should belong to her and then a weird red and black whip like thing lashing out from me and attacking the guys. *That was weird.*

After that I passed out, I think. Then I had the weirdest dream. Michael was there, and I was some magical queen and I needed to save Hell from my evil older sister.

Then we had to meet Bella's dad. As we were leaving, someone attacked us. I couldn't see anything and when I tried to reach for one of the guys, I couldn't move. Then I was pulled against a firm chest and a mystery guy with a sexy ass voice whispered into my ear before everything went black. Damn it, somebody kidnapped me.

Ha. Who would want to kidnap me? I have had the weirdest dreams lately.

Someone must have brought me home after passing out, and I've been sleeping ever since. So, now it's time to get up. I finally peek open my eyes and I see a brown log type ceiling. That's not my room's ceiling, and the warehouse had metal ceilings, not wood.

Fuck. I shoot up to a sitting position and then have to grab my head as pain ricochets around. Damn headache. That wasn't a dream. Someone really kidnapped me. That sexy voice fucker actually drugged me. *Motherfucker.*

My head finally stops beating like some type of war drum cry and I look around the room. I'm on a king-sized bed with black sheets and a black comforter. Twin nightstands sit on either side of the bed, both black as well. A dresser sits across the room and, no surprise, black as well.

Someone likes the color black, don't they? I see two doors, one to my left and the other to my right. One must lead to a bathroom and the other must lead to freedom. *Well, time to leave.*

I crawl out from the mass of blankets that were covering me and realize that once again, someone has changed me. *What the hell?* I'm in a huge, over-sized black t-shirt and from the size of it, the owner is huge as well. Maybe as big as Cas. Shit, the guys must be freaking out.

I don't know how long I've been out, but long enough to know I'm nowhere near my guys. *Wait, not mine.* Actually, they are, huh? Damn it, this is so confusing.

My black and red magic whip claimed them as mine; but what does that really mean? I still have so many questions for Michael.

Well, apparently, my dad. I always wished he was my dad but now it's going to take some getting use to.

"Well, magic, wanna get us out of here?" I whisper to the room, but of course I get no answer. I really wish I knew how to use this magic shit.

I wonder if they have a "How to use magic guidebook", or a "Magic for Dummies" one. That would be super helpful right now. *Focus Azzie.* You can figure this out.

I finally listen to my brain and try the window, but it's one of those that is not meant to open. Ugh. I tiptoe over to the closest door and put my ear to it. I hear nothing, so I try the handle. It gives, and I open it a bit. Bathroom. Okay. Perfect because I actually really have to pee.

I quietly do my business, clean up, and head back to the room. As I start for the other door, I hear footsteps and decide to pretend to be sleeping and get the jump on this guy. I race over to the enormous bed and climb back into my makeshift nest. I close my eyes tightly and wait. *Any minute now.* I hear the creak of the door opening and hear a familiar deep voice.

"I know you're awake, Azzie. You don't have to pretend. I'm certain you have plenty of questions and I can provide the answers." I hear him step into the room, but I don't move.

"I made coffee and breakfast." At the sound of potential food, my trader of a stomach growls and I shoot up in bed and glare at the guy. *Holy hot damn.* I meet the world's darkest color eyes. Black. That's all I see, and it's beautiful, like the nighttime sky full of stars.

"Who the hell are-." Before I can even finish my question, a red and black whip flies out of my chest and wraps itself around this guy's forearm. *You have got to be shitting me. Another one?* What is wrong with me and this damn magic? I'm collecting men like a kid, collects Pokémon cards, gotta catch them all.

"Damn it. I don't even know you." I look up at his face again and see this fucker is grinning, and not like, oh, I'm happy. Oh no, he is grinning like a damn lunatic.

"I knew you would claim me. We're meant to be together, my queen. I will serve you till my last breath." Then, to my horror, he bows.

Okay magic, we need to have a serious conversation about this whole collecting men without my permission thing. They are tasty morsels of men, but what the hell are we supposed to do with six men?

Just as I'm thinking that, an image flashes through my head of a giant bed and all 6 men laying in it, all in stages of undress. I'm so surprised by the image and the fact that I swear I heard a voice whisper "mate" in my head that I don't realize how close to the edge I am and slip off the bed. Before I hit the floor, muscular arms wrap around me.

TWO

KNOX

I surge forward and catch her before she can hit the floor. Gods, she is beautiful, and when I get my hands on that fucker who marked her skin. *Oh, the things my shadows will do to him.*

I hear her intake of breath and decide I better let her go. We have a lot to talk about. I've spent three infuriating years of looking for her. I gently placed her back on the bed and give her a grin. Despite the fact that she does not know who I am in relation to her, her magic still captivates me.

"Look, I don't know who you are and why you decided to kidnap me, but I don't have any money and my five guards or mates or my now boyfriends, I guess. I'm not really sure what to call them since my magic supposedly claimed them as mine kinda like I think I just did to you, but... anyways, not the point. We haven't talked about what this all means for us. So, who the hell are you and why did you kidnap me? I don't think I have the capacity for any more surprises at this time. I just found out recently that I'm not h'm not human. I have no clue about what I am, and I couldn't get the information from Michael because of you kidnapping me. Well, actually he is my dad now. I didn't know he was my dad till recently, but yeah. Oh, and like I said, I have magic and apparently five mates who seem kinda unhinged at times, so if I were you I would let me go."

Holy shit, she is cute. Talking on and on like that. I smile even wider at her. How could I not after that rant?

"Stop smiling like that." She tries to glare at me, but I know I am affecting her like she affects me. I can hear her pounding heart and can smell her need for me in the air.

"You are just too cute. Ranting on like that." She glares hard, but before she can respond, I carry on. "And you have six mates now. I am also a part of your guard." She gives me a confused look. So, I lift my shirt and show her my mark. Her eyes widen and she mumbles something about collecting men like collecting some type of cards.

"So why weren't you with the others if you're a part of my guard and my harem, apparently?" she rolls her eyes at that.

Shit, I don't want to lie to her, but I also don't want her to freak out. I'm sure the other guys have told her horror stories about my kind. *Honesty is key in a good relationship, right?*

I take a deep breath. "I didn't grow up around their kind." She tilts her head as if confused and is trying to figure out what I mean. So, she really knows nothing of the Hell realm. Maybe they haven't told her of my kind.

"So what are you, then?" She asks, but I can see the gears turning in her head. Before I can tell her, she throws herself away from me. "You're — You're the shadow kind. Stay away from me." Shit. I take a step back and raise my hands to show her I mean her no harm.

"Azzie, I would never hurt you. I took you to save you. To keep you safe. Please, you have to believe me."

She starts to shake her head no, but then I remember something. I look down at my arm and see my new mark. I hold out my arm to her. "Look. See. I bare your mark. Your magic knows me. It trusts me. I would never hurt you."

She pauses at that and looks at my arm. "Let's go have some coffee and breakfast and I'll explain some things to you. I'll answer any questions you have as well." She stares at me for a moment, but then nods her head and starts to slowly climb off the bed. I take a step back to make sure she doesn't feel threatened or trapped. She looks up at me and then down at herself. *Shit.* Is she going to be mad that I changed her?

"Ummm, Can I get some pants?" She looks up again and I see a small blush. Ha. I knew I affected her. I walk to the dresser and grab a pair of small sweats that I picked up just for her. She puts them on and looks up at me again.

"So, you obviously know my name, but I have no clue who you are. That's not a great start to this crazy magic chosen relationship, you know." I laugh. Magic chose me right now, but I believe the fates had already written this long before she or I were ever born.

I hold out my hand for her to shake. She grabs it and I feel the tingles of a magical current run up my arm. She grasps like this was the first time she felt them.

"I'm Knox. Prince of one of the shadow kingdoms." I give her a small bow as well. She rolls her eyes. "Ha. Such a gentleman but adding the prince title does nothing for me."

I just shrug. *Had to try.* I swing my arm towards the door. "After you, my queen."

I set a cup of coffee with cream and sugar on the side and she grabs it immediately. She takes a deep breath and then proceeds to dump cream and sugar into her cup. "I'm guessing you like coffee."

"Ha. Do bees like honey? Does yogi bear like picnic baskets? Coffee is the nectar of the Gods. Waits are there actually Gods?" She asks and I nod. "Seriously! Like Zeus and them or like God-God since there is a hell after all?"

I shrug. "Both. But they think they are all better than the other realms and keep to themselves. The story about Heaven and Hell isn't true like the books say. Yes, there is a Heaven, but that is in the angelic realm and a fallen angel did not create Hell." I explain and she just stares at me, like she is expecting me to say just kidding or something. She must realize I'm being serious become she finally nods slowly and takes a sip of her coffee.

"No Shit." she says to herself. Then she hmm as she takes another sip.

"I can tell you more about Hell once we get some food into you. Okay?" She nods again, almost automatically, and I turn back to the stove and make her a plate. I pile up eggs, bacon, and toast, I then make a small bowl of fruit for her. Not what my queen should eat, but the moment I set the plate down, she digs in. At least she seems to like my cooking.

She takes about ten minutes to finish off her plate and I just sit there and smile to myself. This is how it's supposed to be. Me taking care of my queen and making sure she has everything she would ever need.

"Okay, big guy. You're starting to freak me out." She looks up at me and I realize I was just staring at her like a creepy. *Not a good start, Knox.*

I run my hand up the back of my neck. "Oh, sorry about that. I swear I'm not trying to be a creep. You're just so beautiful." She scoffs at me, then rolls her eyes.

"Yeah sure. How about you start talking?" Oh yeah, I really wish I didn't have to explain all this to her, but she needs to know the truth.

"Well, where should I start?" I ask her because really, how do you even go about explaining this all? Plus, she said she just found out about the supernatural kind and that she is actually a long-lost queen.

"Start from the beginning, yeah." I take a deep breath. *Okay. I can do this.*

"Well, as you learned recently, Hell is a realm and in Hell, there are two areas. The area your family is from is called the Royal lands and then there is where I am from. Shadowlands. I promise it is not what everyone thinks. We have three areas and three royal families that rule them. My family rules one of the three areas, making me the heir to the throne. Seventeen years ago, your sister came to the Shadowlands and told my father and the other kings that your mother was planning an attack on our lands. At first, we were confused. Queen Ava had always been a kind and understanding leader. We have never had a problem with her or the Royal lands. Princess Margo said that her mother gave birth to the next true queen and that a seer had seen something terrible. The seer had gone to the queen and told her the shadowland must fall in order for the new queen to rise. Princess Margo told the kings that she didn't think the Shadowlands were a threat and that she wanted to unite and live in peace with us." I take a deep breath because the next part of the story is always the hardest to remember.

"The kings told princess Margo that Queen Ava would do no such thing and that they never had a problem before. They turned her away. That night, a few of the queen's soldiers came to our lands.

They slaughtered two of the kings, a young prince, and all 3 of the queens. My mother included." I hear Azzie's intake of breath and my eyes shoot open. I didn't even release that I had closed them.

"Knox. I'm so sorry." She reaches across the table and places her hand on top of mine and just with that simple touch, I feel a bit of tension in my shoulders relax. "What happened after?" she whispers.

"My father became enraged. He lost his long-time friends and the love of his life. He gathered our armies and sent them to return the favor." I look down for the next part. "Our people slaughtered yours in their sleep. Men, women, children. My father spared but a few. Princess Margo was one of them, but her family had to die. They warned her that if she pulled a move like her mother that he would not show her mercy again. A week later, we held a death rite ceremony for our dead. During the ceremony, a woman came to my father and warned him that not all could be trusted and that he would understand in years to come.

"I never understood either, but my father started to look into the now queen, Margo. He told me once that not all is right in the world and that he could feel the unbalance in the air from time to time."

"I don't understand. It sounds like your father knew something wasn't right. Why is he still working with my wicked witch of a sister? What happened to the other royal families?" she asks in an angry tone and I don't blame her.

"My father took control of the kingdom as the last and remaining king. My father doesn't work with her either. We have to keep up a front. But we never understood why he felt the unbalance until years ago. That's when he remembered a story from before his time."

"What do you mean?" she asks.

"On my 15th birthday, I was with my dad at our lakeside cabin. We were hunting, and I was about to go in for the kill when pain like I have never felt rammed into my chest. I fell to the forest floor and screamed out for my dad. As he approached me, he had a look of horror on his face. I didn't understand why until he explained what the mark on my chest meant. He explained that the queen's mark had claimed me. He was so angry, and I didn't understand why until we got home and he showed me an old book. Hold on, I have it." I get up and head back to the room to grab it. My father told me I had to keep it safe until I found the true queen.

I get back to the kitchen and see Azzie at the sink, washing her dishes. I walk up behind her and reach for them. "A queen should never dirty her hands like this." My chest touches her back and I feel her shiver.

"I am not most queens and I will get dirty if I want." I grin. *No. She is not like most queens, is she?* She leans back towards me, almost like she can't help herself, and I breathe her in. Campfire smoke and warm toasted marshmallows fill my nose and I'm suddenly craving a taste of her in a whole other way.

"Ummm, Knox. Th-the book you were going to get." Book? *Oh yeah*, I shake my head to clear it of the lust filling the air.

"Come sit down and I'll show you." We take our seats at the table and I place the book in front of her and flip to the page I already have marked. "This book holds my people's history and things that were foretold." I glance at her.

"Like a prophecy or something?" She asks and I nod. "Exactly like that."

"Our ancestors predicted this page years before you or I were born. They saw that a queen of the Royal lands would unite our people in a union. When Princess Margo came to our leaders, they thought she could be the one, but they were wrong. Look here." I point to the image on the page of a girl facing away from the reader with dark hair that fades to red and a mark on her back. The mark is of a pentagram in a circle with a crescent moon on either side of it and six stars that sit atop the pentagram. It's a beautiful piece of work and it's the same mark that claims my queen's back and my chest.

"Is that who I think it is?" she whispers and I nod because what else do I say? "No. You're telling me that I'm not only the queen of Hell, but I'm supposed to unite two people who sort of kind of hate each other right now." I nod again.

"I know this is a lot to take in, but my father has been trying to find you to protect you. I know you have little to go on, but your sister has been deceiving both our kingdoms for many years. If we don't stop her soon, all of Hell will fall." She looks at me wide eye.

Damn it.

THREE

CAS

What the hell is happening?

"Azzie." I yell out into the cloying smoke. "Who has eyes on Azzie?" I hear coughing to my left and head towards that person. A few steps in, and I bump into Remi. I can barely see him and he is less than a foot in front of me right now.

"Where is she?" I ask again. *This can't be happening.* We just got her and now this.

Remi coughs out again. "No. I think she was next to Kam?" I hear more coughing to my right and head in that direction next.

This time I find Max. "What the hell is this stuff?" he asks while trying to clear the air in front of him with his hand. The effort is pointless since the smoke is so murky in the air.

"I have no idea. It's like smoke, but almost thicker. Where was Azzie last?" I take a deep breath by accident and almost choke on how dense this stuff is. It almost feels like it is coating my throat in a layer of slime.

I keep moving. Locating Azzie is my priority. I have one job, to protect the queen and this isn't the first time I have failed.

I hear Kam in front of me, calling out for Azzie as well. *Shit.* Wasn't she supposed to be with him?

"Kam. Where the fuck is she? She was with you. Where did she go?" I growl out. My demon starting to surface with every minute that passes and we don't have Azzie in our sight.

"I-cough- don't-cough- know-cough. She was right here. The smoke hit, and I went to grab her, but the smoke was already so thick. Azzie!" He yells out for her again.

"Azzie. Baby girl. If you don't answer me this second, I swear I will turn you ass redder than the tips of your hair." If Azzie was near she would answer me after calling her out like this, but I already know the truth. Someone took her, but the real question is who.

"Shadows." I turn around and Cain is there. The smoke has finally thinned enough and I can see his enormous form now. "What?" I ask because I don't think I heard him right.

"Shadows. It's not smoke. It's shadow." I stare at him, not fully ready to admit that we failed. We have trained all of our lives and we failed to protect the one person who could save our home. Who could save us.

The shadows start to flow in the direction of the warehouse door and as I look to the reason; I see Michael sucking the shadows into his chest. Which could only mean one thing. I don't think. I shift and grab Michael by the throat, lifting him an inch or two off the ground.

"It was you. Everything you told us was bullshit. Where is she?" I growl centimeters from his face. To my surprise, though, he just lets me manhandle him. Like I'm not seconds away from crushing his windpipe or snapping his neck. I fell a hand land on my shoulder and I glance at the person who wants to join Michael on the wrong side of my rage.

"Brother, he needs air to tell us what he knows. Loosen your hold."
I growl back at Cain. How dare he try to take Michael's death away
from me. *He is the reason I don't have my queen to worship.* The
reason Azzie was taken away from us. *Again.*

Shit. I actually have feelings for Azzie and I already lost her before
I could tell her. Before, I could show her.

Michael wheezes out something, and I finally loosen my hold. *I
suppose Cain is right.* I need to know how to find her and who I
need to kill. Slowly. Painfully.

I drop this worthless man on the ground. "Talk." He raises his
hands in the air and I think he is going to attack, but then I realize he
sucks more of the remaining shadow back into himself. He coughs
some more, and the Birdy walks up and holds out a hand to him.

"No." Birdy turns towards me. "Boy, you do not know the entire
story. You must listen." She can't be serious. We get attacked by
shadows and Michael can control them. *Last I checked, one plus one
equals two.*

Michael stands and wipes the dirt from his clothes. "Come inside.
We need to talk. I should have told you all this before. I thought we
had time. Azzie has been through so much." A chill runs up my back
and I have a feeling we aren't ready for what he is about to tell us. He
turns around and walks back into the warehouse, followed by Birdy.
My brother's approach and we all stand there for a second, looking
after them.

"What do you think he is going to tell us?" Remi asks, but I think
he already knows as well.

"Only one way to find out." I reply.

The faster we figure this all out. The faster we find Azzie and bring
her home. Where she belongs.

FOUR

AZZIE

I stare at Knox wide eyed. He can't be serious. Haven't these guys heard of too much pressure? It's been a month and my world has become something I don't even recognize and half the time can believe. Who would?

When I was younger, I used to wish upon stars and daydream about being a princess who needed to be saved by the handsome prince. This is not what I had in mind. As I grew up, and then met Michael, well my dad, I learned princesses don't need a prince to save them. Sometimes you just got to save yourself, but it seems fate had other plans for me.

That bitch was like, "oh hey Azzie, so remember all those wishes you made about prince charm. Well, you see, I was saving them for now so, here's six men who you probably want to kill half the time, but you're totally in love with them." Whoa there. *Love. No. I couldn't love these guys.* I barely tolerate them most days, but then that warm little flame that I've come to realize as my magic, pops her little head up and I can about see the look on her little face. Basically saying "you're in denial Azzie. You know you feel things for them." *Can magic even have a face or this much attitude?*

"Azzie." Knox calls to me and I realize I must have zoned out. "I know this is a lot, but you have me to help you through this all."

"What about the others?" He cocks an eyebrow at me. "I know this sounds weird because I barely know any of you, but my skin feels itchy and I get this feeling, like my magic is calling to be near them." His silent for a second before he finally responses.

"Lets lie low for a few days and then we can reach out to them. The man that raised you, Frank, he knows where you are. He will send more men to hunt you down. Most of the shadow kind still follow your sister's rule. They do not know of her deceit, but they will. Until then, we must keep you safe till you turn eighteen and come into full power." I eye him. *Can I really trust this guy?* He did just kidnap me, but my magic did say he was ours. *I think.*

Going off topic, I decide I need answers about a few things. "Can magic have a face? Is it supposed to have so much attitude? I mean, I think it's attitude, that's the vibe I get. Is it like a living thing inside of me, because I did not give it permission to claim a bunch of men. I was joking when I said I wanted a harem of men." Okay, I kind of wanted a harem, but I didn't think it would happen. Knox gives me an odd look and then laughs. "What? I'm being serious."

"Yes, yes. I know. It's just, I've never had to explain this to someone before. I've never known a supernatural that didn't know what they were." He laughs a bit more before he sobers up and takes a deep breath. "Your magic is a part of you. Since the day you were born. It's always been there. At fifteen, supes get their magic unlocked. You, on the other hand, are different. As the marked queen, you are one of the most powerful supernatural born. Your magic was partially unlock at fifteen, but the rest will remain locked until your eighteenth birthday. I'm not sure what this Michael or your other men explained to you yet."

"They touched bases on that. My sister thinks she can steal my power on my eighteenth, and that's why she wants me. I was told that I would have a few years to bond with my guard but that now I only have a few weeks. How am I supposed to bond with them if I can't be near them?" This doesn't feel right. I feel like I'm missing something being away from them. *How can that even be possible?*

"What about my magic feeling like it has a mind of its own? You said it's a part of me, but it doesn't feel like it. I get these images and feelings that don't feel like my own." I say because my magic serious just rolled her eyes at me like I'm being dense or something.

Knox chuckles but abruptly stops when I glare at him. This is serious. He holds up his hands like I might attack him. *He's not wrong.* "Your magic is a part of you. It is you. It is also not a part of you." What?

"What do you mean? That makes no sense." Knox gets up and goes to a drawer in the kitchen and grabs something out. When he gets back to the table, I realize it's a piece of paper and a pen. This is not the time for art class.

"Okay, let me see if I can explain better." I tilt my head to the side, wondering where the hell this is going. He draws a circle and then writes my name in the center. Then he draws another circle, overlapping the one he just drew. Then labels this one magic. Where the circles overlap, he writes the word soul. I think I'm even more confused now.

"This circle is you, mind, body and soul." He points to the first circle and my soul section. I nod. He points to the magic circle. "This is your magic. It is a part of your soul, but it also has a slight mind of its own."

"So, it's like another person is inside of me." I ask because nope. *Won't do that. Get it out.*

"What? No, not like a person. How do I explain this better? So, you know how some of your other men can shift?" I nod. Kam and Cain are hellhounds. Maxwell is a dragon, Remi is a fae, incubus mix, but I don't think he can shift. Cas, well, Cas is a demon. I haven't seen him fully shifted, but I saw little horns and grayish skin that day at the back of the school.

"Well, their shifted form is like another person. It's their magic. But it's also ingrained into their DNA." Okay, so that makes sense. *I think.*

"Wait, I don't have a shifted form, though." At least I don't think I do. He lifts an eyebrow at my comment.

"No way. Do I? What do I shift into?" I try to picture myself shifting into something, anything, but nothing comes to mind and I deflate a bit. I feel my magic shift again, but instead of becoming something remarkable, I get a look of annoyance from her. I have never encountered anyone or anything with such a sassy attitude before.

"I actually don't know. You're not a normal supernatural, so it could be anything, really." He gives me a smile and I slump more into my chair. *I'm even a freak among the supernatural.* "But you should find out when you turn eighteen. I promise."

"How do I control my magic, then? I have enough men. I don't need any more." But I can't ignore the fact I still feel like I'm missing something right now. Like I'm not whole. An ache in my chest crying out for something and I think I might know what. Or who.

"Well, it's never been heard of a marked queen ever having more than four guardsmen. I believe your mother had four and others have had three. It is believed that the more guardsmen a queen has, the more powerful the queen will be." He looks at me from across the table while I process that I'm once again a freak. *So, I collect guys like Pokémon cards and that makes me more powerful. Outstanding.* My magic peeks up and winks at me. Ugh. We do not need any more men. We can barely deal with the ones we have. I swear she shrugs, like this is no big deal.

How the hell am I supposed to keep six guys happy? I've never even been with one, and now I'm supposed to entertain six. Not possible. Nope. Not going to happen, plus I've seen Max naked and, ummm, that's not going to fit. I can't even imagine what the others could be packing underneath their pants. An image pops into my head of me on a bed, bare to all with all six guys around me, reaching for me and...

"Azzie! Are you okay? You zoned out for a minute." Knox waves a hand in front of my face and I just know my cheeks have turned bright red now. *What is wrong with me?* I feel my magic giggle. Actually, giggles like a naughty little girl who just got caught and thinks it's funny.

"Can someone's magic make them see stuff in their head?" I ask, confused because there is no way that was my thought. Knox cocks an eyebrow in question, wanting me to continue, but I stay quiet. Then, like a lightbulb going off, a smirk graces his stupidly sexy face.

"I see. Magic can be, what's a good word, primal. Magic wants to be with their soul mates so, it might try to convince you with images or feelings. It happens to all of us." He smiles bigger and now my face has to be as red as a tomato. I look away like I wasn't just thinking of wanting to climb this guy like a jungle gym. Stupid horny magic.

"So, where are we exactly?" I look around, but nothing looks familiar. "When can I contact the guys to let them know I'm not dead? I'm sure they are freaking out. They really are kind of possessive." Once again, my magic makes herself known by doing a little shimmy like their possessive attitudes excite her. For something that has been with me for years without me knowing, she sure is making herself known now.

"I know you want to be near them, but I don't think it's such a good idea." He doesn't look at me when he says this. "Why not?"

"My father told me he overheard your sister say she has someone in town watching you and reporting back to her. He doesn't know who, and we have been trying to figure it out, but it's not safe." He looks over at me this time and I can see the honesty in his face, but I can just leave them.

"Look, I know you want to protect me, but I will never bow to another person ever again and I won't run scared because my wicked bitch of a sister thinks she should have the family crown. If I really am meant to be the queen of Hell, I guess I need to start now. Right?" I straighten my shoulders and lift my head higher. I almost feel like I need to practice my princess wave like in Princess Diaries.

"Azzie, I rea-" He stops talking when I give him a "don't you dare argue with me" glare.

"I am not weak, Knox. If I keep hiding from the big bad wolf, then that is exactly what I am. I won't be a scared little girl anymore. The only way someone can hurt me is if I let them. Plus, I have six big, powerful men to protect me if I can't handle something. Now, if you think I'm weak and can't be queen, then tell me now." I smile inwardly because I've seen enough movies to know, when you tell a guy to disagree with you, they won't because women are crazy and it's smarter to just agree with them than to argue.

He takes a deep breath and I see the exact moment I won. "Your right." Ha. *See. Men are intimidated by women.*

"Great. Now take me to my other men and let's explain what is going on."

FIVE

KAM

I can feel the heavy weight of failure again as we enter the warehouse. *Why can't we keep her protected?* We have trained all of our lives for this and a month into meeting her; we have failed multiple times. First, by allowing Bella to even speak to Azzie the way she did. Second, the night at the club when the shadow kind attacked her. Third, when Bella decided to pull that stunt while stealing Azzie's clothes. Then seeing all those scars. Someone abused my angel, and we never knew. Now someone has taken her away from us, again. The shadow kind, if the black smoke like air was any indication. Plus, we might have a traitor right in front of us. Michael. Someone who Azzie seemed to trust is a shadow kind being.

We enter the living room where less than an hour ago Azzie was safe with us. I look around just in case she might have run back in here, but I already know she is not anywhere near us. Grim whines in my head evening louder, like if he whines loud enough I will know where she is. But we haven't fully bonded yet. Yes, she claimed us, but she doesn't trust us enough to bond on a deeper level. *That bond would have been useful right now.*

Michael walks over to the couch and takes a seat, still rubbing at his throat where a bruise is starting to appear. Cas wasn't playing around when he saw Michael absorb the shadows into himself outside. Birdy walks over to him and gives him a sad look but nods. "Now boys, I need you all to stay calm and hear Michael out. What he is about to tell you can't leave this room and shouldn't be revealed until the right time. Azzie's life depends on it." She gives us all a serious look and we all nod. The moment she said Azzie's life depended on it, we were all ready to do whatever it took.

"Mac, Ivy, Caleb, that goes for you all as well. Azzie will need you three the most soon. You must be strong for her." She looks over at Azzie's three best friends and they all look at each other before nodding as well. "Caleb, would you seal the room for us, please?" Caleb looks around, then walks to the middle of the room. He waves his hands through the air and mumbles something. He looks around once more, nods to himself, then walks back to where the two girls are.

The five of us mates all stand in front of Michael waiting for his explanation but also ready to attack if we don't like what we hear. Azzie would forgive us if she knew her dad was a traitor and set her up. Worse, if he allowed her to be sent to her sister. What would happen to her then? *No. I think of that.*

Michael clears his throat. "Azzie is not just the true queen of hell, but in order for you to understand, I have to explain some things. Take a seat." He gestures to the chairs around the room, but none of us moves. We wouldn't believe a word he says if it wasn't for Birdy asking us to listen. He looks down as if he is saddened by the fact that we won't trust him, but I don't care. We should be out there looking for Azzie, but no, we have to pretend we are in kindergarten and have story time and waste valuable time we could be using to find her.

"I know you all will not understand at first, but keep an open mind." he pauses to take a deep breath before continuing, "Years ago, before any of you were even born, Queen Ava, Azzie's mother, wanted to have a good relationship with the Shadowlands. She wanted to open up the kingdoms and allow for a peace agreement and trade route to be opened. See, the kingdoms were never at war, but we never had an official agreement. Stories of the scary Shadowlands were made to keep peace between kingdoms. Beware of the big vicious beasts that live among the shadows." He rolls his eye as he says this. "These rumors were created long before anyone could remember, but royal families knew the truth. But queen Ava, well she had a beautiful soul and wanted to create a peaceful land through the whole of Hell. So, queen Ava invited the three Shadowland royal families to dinner and a meeting to talk about what they could do to open up boarders so that everyone knew the truth." He looks down then and takes a deep breath. When he looks back up, I can see a small smile, like he is remembering that day. "I was known as King Michael Morningstar at that time and had never met the queen of the Royal Lands but, the moment I saw her I knew I belonged to her. She had three guardsmen that had already bonded with her, but the second our eyes met it must have been written in the fates that I would serve her till my last breath." His smile drops and I start to get a picture of what he is trying to tell us, but it's not possible. Well, never been heard of.

"Since we were from two different lands, we knew it would not be easy to be together. She had her duties, and I had mine. We met in secret often. It was so hard to be away from her. We could only go so many days until our magic would force us to be near each other. After a few weeks of this, her magic marked me." He pulls up his shirt and shows us the queen's mark that belongs to queen Ava. My eyes widen. A Royal Land being mating with a Shadowlands, never in the history of Hell has this happened. It's said that mating with a Shadowland being would corrupt your magic. Then I remember Azzie's magic. Red and black. So, she's...

"A week after queen Ava and I mated she became pregnant, but we never thought I was the father. We assumed one of the others was the father. We were happy regardless. She had already had Margo and Jasper, and I was just happy to have a family. So, I stepped away from the throne and passed it to my younger brother. They did not know me outside of my kingdom and Ava and her guard, so we decided I would hide my shadows and step up as a mate from the earth realm. We would say that we met on one of her trips to the realm. A month before Azzie was born, Birdy came to us and told us Azzie would hold power and that someone was going to try to take it. So, we came up with the plan we told you about earlier. We still did not know who held her other half of DNA, but on the night Azzie came into the world, we knew." He stares up at us, imploring us to understand, but I'm speechless. I had a feeling this was coming, but hearing it was something else.

"Azzie is half Royal Land and half Shadowland. She is the first of her kind and holds more power than anyone could imagine."

I stand there with the others in utter shock. For the first time in what feels like forever, Remi is completely speechless. Azzie is half Shadowland. Does she know? Why didn't we know? Cas must be thinking the same thing because he turns to Birdy with a glare.

"Did you know?" She nods her head once. "Wouldn't that have been important for us to have known? To know that our true queen is part Shadowkind." I turn and look at my other brothers, then turn back to Cas. *What is he trying to say? Would that change how I feel about her? Probably not.*

"Would that have affected your perception of Azzie? Would you have trained so hard and been prepared to give your life for her if you knew?" Birdy stands and walks towards us. "If the circumstances had been different, and you knew, would you have altered the way you had to go in order to save your home and guard your queen?" She stops in front of Cas. "I found out when Azzie got to town. Azzie is a miracle, Cas. Never have Royal Lands or Shadowlands mated before. This will change the history of Hell, but Azzie does not know of her true power yet." Cas scoffs.

"This changes everything." He hisses out and turns his glare on Michael. "Your kind slaughtered ours in the middle of the night. They killed families as they slept and who were of no threat to them." Cas goes to take a step toward him, but luckily Cain and Max step in front of him.

"Cas. You need to calm down. Listen to what they have to say. Then we decide what to do but Azzie needs us right now." Max says in a calm tone but it seems Cas is hearing none of it.

"Azzie needs us. Ha. She is probably a part of all this." Kam growls at Cas and honestly, I want to too. He can't be serious. She didn't even know about supernatural's.

"Do you know what powers queen Margo possess?" Michael asks out of nowhere. At first, his question throws me off, but then I realize that none of us know. The Royal Lands never talked about the royal family's magic. We all knew they were stronger than the rest of the supernatural kind and had special gifts, but never of what magic they could hold. I see the realization in everyone's eyes and Cas shakes his head, seeming almost confused now by the change of subject.

"Queen Ava was trying to unite the lands for over a year back then and was in good standings to make that happen. Margo had gone to the Shadowlands on the day Azzie was born. She told us she wanted to get a gift for her younger sister. She wanted to get a blessed stone from our land. It is said you make a wish and give the stone to a loved one for protection. At the time, we did not know what Margo was truly up to. Birdy had seen a takeover and many things, but never who or when they would. Margo went there that day not to bless Azzie but to condemn her." He looks around the room and then takes a deep breath. "Back then, we knew Margo had exceptional skills in spells. She takes after her father as a witch after all, but she got ahold of a dark magic book. One that shouldn't have existed, and that taught things like death magic. She had learned to bewitch people. She had gone to the Shadowlands and made them truly believe Queen Ava was planning an attack and that they should attack first before the Royal Lands could." He looks down then. "We never knew that Margo had sent men to kill the Shadowland royal families. Her attack killed my brother, his wife, and many others." I can hear the saddest in his voice and the pain in his eyes.

"When I saw what was to happen, I started the plan to fake Michael's death. I knew we could not save all of our people that night. If we tried, then there would not have been a Hell to save today. It would have been a war that would have slaughtered many on both sides. Azzie may be half Shadowland, but she is the bridge that will unite both lands and restore Hell to what it once was, only greater. You see, boys, Azzie is not just the queen of Hell for the Royal Land. She is the rightful queen of the Hell realm as a whole. There is so much more to the Hell realm than you all have been taught." Birdy says dropping that little bomb in our laps. Cas stands there in a daze, as if he can't quite believe what he is hearing. *Me either, brother.*

Remi, being who he is, finally gets back to himself and breaks the seriousness in the room. "Holy shit. You're telling me that my mate is the queen of all queens? I knew she was badass, but this is a whole other level." He grins wide, and as I think about it, he's right. I knew Azzie was special, but this is extra special. My brother, on the other hand, has to be the one that sees reason and brings us all back to a stark reality.

"If Azzie is this queen of all queens, the fate of Hell is in even more danger. My question now is, where is Azzie and who took her?" *Shit.*

"The bigger question is, does Margo have her?" Max asks, sending a chill down my back and making Grim growl out. *Double shit.*

I hear a throat clear behind me and turn to see Azzie's friends step up. "She's not in Hell." Mac says.

"How the fuck do you know that?" Cas demands and Mac rolls her eyes.

"You're an idiot. She bonded us, remember?" We all glance at one another. Does that mean they know where she's at?

"Where is she then?" Max asks this time. Caleb speaks this time. "We don't know where, but she didn't go far. Her energy is strong just being blocked somehow. So, we can't get a location." Grim whines again in my head. He is jealous that we haven't bonded and that her friends have a better connection to her than us. *Same buddy, same.*

"Then who the fuck took her?" Cas demands. He starts to pace but after a few minutes, stops abruptly. "That motherfucker." Then takes off towards the door.

What motherfucker?

Six

CAIN

I watch for a moment as Cas paces back and forth. What is he doing? We need to go find Azzie. If what Michael told us is true, Azzie is in even more danger than we thought. He stops abruptly and lets out a curse. *Does he know who took her?* Reaper whines in my head.

"That motherfucker." Then he starts for the door. I call after him but he is so focused on going after this person he thinks is behind Azzie going missing. We don't even know who he is thinking did this, but sharing with the class would be nice.

As if we were one, the rest of us follow behind Cas. Max, usually being the calm one, gets to Cas first. "Hey man, why don't you slow your roll and tell us what's going on?" He places his hand on Cas shoulder but Cas just shakes it off.

"Don't you all see it!" He turns and faces us and with his face twisted in rage. Placing my hands up to show him we aren't the problem here; I take a step forward. "Cas, man. This isn't you. What don't we see? Who do you think did this?" I say as calmly as possible. Cas's demon is on the edge of a full shift if the eye and skin color shifting is any indication.

Cas looks me in the eye, and I see the moment he realizes some-thing. He bows his head and ever so quietly, he says, "It's my fault. I've been against her the whole time. I pushed her away from us. We could have been bonded by now, but I lost hope she was real. Now, someone has taken her and it's all my fault." At first, I'm stunned because I just heard Cas be something other than confident. Remi, reigning in his shock once again, first grabs Cas by the shoulder in an awkward side hug.

"It's not just your fault, Cas. We all ignored the way we were being called to her. You weren't the only one who had lost hope. Now is not the time to self-pity ourselves. Azzie needs us. Who were you about to go kill, anyway?" Well, Remi was doing great till the end. I roll my eyes.

"Who wanted Azzie out of the picture? Who might be angry that she won't bow down to them?" I quirk an eyebrow at him. Does he really think Bella of all people could be the mastermind behind this? I know the chick is crazy, but crazy enough to kidnap Azzie.

"Dude, Bella is not that bright." Remi says with a laugh. He has a point. Her dad has to pay the teachers to give her good grades. She thinks because she is pretty that she shouldn't have to be smart, too. She even thinks that one day the five of us will wake up and be madly in love with her. Ha.

"No. Not Bella. Her dad. He wanted to meet with her alone and then out of nowhere we are attacked and she goes missing. Bella could have told her dad anything and with Azzie claiming us in front of her, she is probably even more pissed. I can only imagine what her mind came up with to tell the mayor." Cas tells us and when I think about it, he's right. The mayor is all about power, so if Bella told him that Azzie made a fool of her and that she needed to be taken care of, he could have done something. He is just as delusional as his daughter. He thinks we plan to be Bella's mates as well. The whole family is crazy. But then the real question is, how did he get ahold of the shadows?

"Cas, this all makes sense, but the shadows. How do you explain someone using shadows? No one is dumb enough to work with a shadow kind, right?" Max voices my thoughts. I look over at Michael.

"What do you think?" I ask him. Him being from the Shadowland's could be useful. "Could the mayor be working with the Shadowlands?" He takes a second to think about it, but then slowly nods his head.

"It's possible. Margo has been looking for Azzie for years. She has probably tried to use other seers as well. She could have offered money or power to those who found her. Do not underestimate Margo or the Shadowlands." We all look at each other. Would the mayor really make a deal with Shadowlands? I mean, we know now that the rumors of their kind and land aren't actually true, but I doubt others know the truth.

"I guess we need to pay Bella and her dad a visit. Don't you think?" Cas looks around and I'm pretty sure our expressions match his. *Time to go find our queen.*

Just as I thought he would, Cas doesn't bother to knock. He simply turns the knob and walks right into the mayor's office. Sure enough,

Bella is sitting on his couch across the room. When she sees us, she jumps up and pastes a fake smile on her face..

"Oh Cas. You finally showed up. Now we can talk about removing that stupid mark on your arm." Five growls come out from around the room at her statement. *She cannot be serious right now.*

"Bella! Sit down." Mr. Blackwood hisses at his daughter. Bella turns towards him and pouts. Honest to the god's pouts. "I'm sorry, gentlemen. Please have a seat." He looks around the room and frowns. "I'm sorry, but can I ask where miss Mornings is? I was told she would be here with you, all. That is what this meeting is about." When none of us move or says anything, he takes a seat and calls out to Beta James. "James. Did you not tell me that the girl would be coming to have a conversation?" James nods his head, then looks around in confusion.

"Tell me Blackwood." Cas starts and Bella's dad grinds his teeth at the fact that we don't call him by his alpha title. *Like any of us care, he is an alpha.* "Do you have any idea where Azzie Mornings is?" The mayor's eyes crinkle in confusion. "I would think very carefully about your answer, if I were you." Cas warns in an ice cold tone.

He stands again and places his hands on the desk in front of him. "What are you talking about, boy?" Cas growls at the term boy. He steps forward and his skin starts to fade to a dull gray that shows his demon is near the surface. Mr. Blackwood raises his hands in defense. He knows who the real predators are in this room. "I mean no disrespect, but I'm not sure what you mean by your questions. I was told miss Mornings would be coming to meet with me and was bringing some type of guard." He looks over at his beta and Bella then returns his eyes to us.

I glance over at my brother. He has been relatively quiet since Azzie went missing and I'm just waiting for him to snap. Grim had been the closest to Azzie and, with her nowhere to be found, it must be driving him up the wall. Similar to the rest of us, I'm sure, but our beasts do not understand that we can't just tear people apart to find her. Reaper flashes me an image of bodies spread out across the floor. *Obviously, he disagrees.*

Max steps up next to Cas and speaks next. "Shadows so thick we couldn't see through them ambushed us as we were leaving our home. Once they disappeared, Azzie was nowhere to be found." My head snaps to the couch where Bella lets out a giggle like this is all fun and games for her.

"Blackwood, I would suggest you control your daughter. She has already made a fool of herself and we will not take anymore disrespect towards our missing mate." Cas says in a deadly calm voice. After his bold statement of assuming Azzie will still want us after we failed once again to keep her safe, you could hear a pin drop. This must surprise the alpha, because he seems generally surprised by this news.

"Ah, Bella didn't tell you. Your daughter has been starting quite a bit of drama lately." Remi adds with a chuckle. Bella jumps up and stomps her foot like an unhappy child.

"Daddy, that bitch claimed them without permission and they were already courting me before that trash showed up. It's not fair. They are mine." Bella whines and my most laid back of brother's snaps. Remi's magic swirls and then shoots out, grabbing Bella by the neck. I can tell he didn't want to kill her because his grip wasn't all that tight, but he meant business. As I glanced over at him, I realized he was using his fae magic for the first time in a while, but he also has a confused look on his face. *Odd.*

"Bella. We warned you. Keep my mate's name out of your mouth." Bella is grasping for air now and starts reaching toward Remi's magic, but keeps swatting at air instead of a solid form. He laughs then, but it's not a friendly laugh, no it's a crazed laugh that says he will kill her with a snap of her neck.

"Remi, please release my daughter. I will deal with her disrespect myself." Blackwood glances back and forth between Bella and Remi. Remi looks over at Cas and, when he nods in return, Remi releases his hold on Bella's throat and she drops to the floor, coughing. Tears start to run down her cheeks, ruining her makeup. A tiny part of me feels bad at first, but then Reaper flashes a picture of Azzie standing in the school's hallway naked and the tiny feeling vanishes.

"Daddy. I didn't do anything wrong. They were mine first." She says to her dad, then turns to look over at us. "She bewitched you guys. Why can't you see that?" This time it's her dad that growls out at her.

"Silence Bella. You have embarrassed me and yourself enough. James, take Bella to her room and keep her there until I've decided what to do with her." James goes and gently picks Bella up and walks towards the door, but as he starts to walk past, an icy chill runs down my spine. I look at my brother across from me and he must have got the same feeling because he eyes James with suspicion. Something is not right with him. But does it have anything to do with Azzie going missing? He was there right before she was taken. I'm about to voice my opinion, but Cas starts to speak.

"Blackwood. I would keep your daughter in line from now on. You have allowed her to run free for long enough. If she continues to go after our mate, we will have no choice but to deal with her ourself. She underestimates Azzie, but before we get into that, we must make a magical binding agreement that what is said here today shall not be spoken outside this room. Do you understand?" Mr. Blackwood takes a moment to straighten himself, then looks Cas in the eyes and nods once. He walks around the desk and stands in front of us.

"I, Johnathan Blackwood, here by swear my silence of what is spoken of here today and forevermore, for if I fail, so does my mind." He takes his hand and lengthens a single claw and slices his palm. Cas does the same and then they shake each other's hand. Cas's magic wraps around their joined hands and seems to fade into Mr. Blackwood's palm. Now if he speaks of anything said, Cas will know.

Cas looks around the room, making eye contact with each of us. "Blackwood, you should have a seat for this conversation." Then, using our bond, he speaks to us.

"He isn't involved. I can tell by his magic. So, the only thing I can think of is to bring him into the loop. Maybe he might know something, like someone new or things that have been happening."

"We have been occupied with other matters lately. We could have missed something." Max speaks next.

"Exactly, but do we have time to sit here and chat? We need to find Azzie. What if she is hurt?" Kam says in a frustrated tone. Seems like Grim is getting to him. Well, he has lasted longer than I thought he would.

"I'm with Kam. What if Margo has her already?" Remi, for once not sounding so laid back.

"Look, I know we all want to find her, but we have no leads other than someone who used shadows. Blackwood might know something and not realize it. Plus, we know Azzie is not injured. We may not be bonded fully yet, but we would still know that through our guard's mark. Keep ahold of yourselves. Azzie needs us to stay focused and calm. Now let's drop a bomb of a lifetime on Blackwood's Day." Then with a serious look towards the mayor, "Blackwood, do you really know who your daughter has been threatening?"

SEVEN

AZZIE

Three days! 72 hours! 4320 minutes since I've seen my guys and yes, I mean my guys, because being away from them has been awful. After the first day, I started to feel itchy and uncomfortable in my skin. There was an enormous weight on my chest and I didn't understand why until day two. That's when my magic started to send me images of the guys and then the pieces fell into place.

I told Knox that I needed to go to them and that I thought it was making me sick. He seemed concerned but told me to wait just a few more days till he could come up with a better plan to keep me safe. I rolled my eyes because I can keep myself safe, but I agreed because if what he says is true, my crazy ass sister will stop at nothing to get to me and that includes killing the guys.

If you had asked me a week ago if I felt anything for them, I would have laughed in your face. I mean, I thought the guys were hot and all and even joked about having them as a harem, but now I realize that I actually liked them.

Kam, the sweet and quiet Hellhound who cuddles in bed and helps keep the nightmares away.

Cain, Kam's twin, is always watching and taking mental notes. I know he is super smart because he always has a book in his hands; it seems like. But when I had both my hellhounds in bed to cuddle, I felt truly safe for the first time in years.

Then there is my charming incubus, fae playboy. He has the looks and the smooth talking that every girl daydreams about at least once. He totally fits the incubus attitude that I've heard of, but he makes me laugh and not the fake kind.

Max, at first, was an unknown to me. He was nice when we worked together, kept his eyes on me. Then we had to work together in class, and that's when I started to notice he would become anxious around me. Almost like he couldn't wait to get away from me. Come to find out his dragon likes my smell a little too much.

Cas, on the other hand, has always been a love- hate relationship. I mean, he is great to look at and his mere presence could almost command an entire room. He is a bit of a control freak, but I secretly want to see what happens when I make him lose that tightly held control.

Last but not least, my newest mate, Knox. I met him days ago, but the last few days would have been even worse if he wasn't here. Knox is sweet and caring and cooks amazing food. He is as big as Cas but he has brightly colored red hair and when he uses his shadows, his eyes turn a deep red shade as well. They are almost black without them.

The last few nights, Knox has been sleeping right outside of the room. He thinks I don't know, but I have been barely sleeping as well. Too afraid of the nightmares coming back and this restless feeling of being empty.

I'm sitting on the couch as Knox walks in with more firewood. It's late fall here, so it becomes a bit chilly when the sun goes down. I look up at him and then I realize my mistake. *Why is he shirtless?*

That should be a crime because hot damn, I want to lick him like a lollipop. I shake my head at that crazy thought because no Azzie; it is not appropriate to lick someone. *But I suppose if I lick it, it's mine.*

He glances over and as if he knew where my mind went; he gives me a smirk then crooks his eyebrow in question.

Shit, am I drooling or something? I rip my eyes away and pretend my magic is not flashing images of my bed with Knox naked above me, kissing my neck and then moving...Nope. *Damn horny magic.*

To get my mind away from those thoughts and on something else, I look outside the little living room window. The cabin that Knox brought us to is actually kind of cute. It's a log-built style with a small porch out front and two old white rocking chairs that sit to the side. When you enter the front door, it's open and airy, with the living room to the left and the dining room and kitchen to the right. There is a long hallway just at the back of the open space that leads to four bedrooms. Two smaller ones that each fit a queen mattress and some furniture. The last bedroom is the master suite. Although the bed I woke up in feels like heaven, it's still not as nice as being with my hellhounds. The place has two bathrooms, one between the two spare rooms and then the master has its own with the biggest bathtub I have ever seen. I haven't used it yet, but it's on my to do list.

This cabin is what I picture when I think of a nice little getaway with the family. A pang goes through my chest because I don't really have a family, do I? My mom and her guard are prisoners. I think Michael said I had a brother, but who knows if he is like my crazy evil sister and wants me dead too. Michael is my dad apparently, but I'm still upset that he knew who I was this whole time and never said a thing. I suppose the guys are my family now, since you know, I mated to them. I'm wondering if they recognize there is an additional sixth mate to add to my collection. I've come to regard Mac, Ivy and Caleb as family too. So maybe I do have a family, but what are they doing right now? I sigh and it must have been out loud, because Knox looks over at me again and frowns.

"What's wrong, my queen?" He asks and comes over to sit next to me. I lift my shoulders in response because he already knows. If this feeling of being empty keeps intensifying, I will need the guys soon. I haven't told Knox yet, but I feel like I'm wasting away. I can barely walk or even move without feeling pain shoot through my body. It is only from years of practice that I can keep in my grimace every time I move. He looks out the window and his frown deepens. I'm about to ask him what is wrong when he snaps his head down to me and smiles.

"How about some fresh air? Maybe a picnic? I know this cute clearing we could go to and just relax. It's not that far and I could carry you if you get tired." He says in a sheepish tone while run his hand down the back of his neck and I giggle a little at how nervous he seems to be.

"A picnic sounds nice and so does some fresh air. How about you go work on lunch and I'll go change." He nods his head and then leans over and kisses my forehead. I smile a little because every time he touches me, the pain eases just a little.

It doesn't take him long to get a picnic basket and lunch ready. I finish changing just as he sets everything by the door. "Are you ready, my queen? I can carry you as well." I laugh.

"I can walk just fine, thank you." He glances at me like he knows I'm in pain, but I crook my brow but he just looks away and grabs the basket, then opens the door. The fresh air hits my face and I inhale the fresh pine scent.

"After you, my queen." He does a little bow and I roll my eyes.

He was right about it not being far, but with my body hurting the way it is, it takes us an extra few minutes. I pretend to be sightseeing and just enjoying the fresh air and sunshine on my skin, but I can tell he never takes his eyes off me like he thinks I will collapse at any second.

Once at the clearing, he sets up a blanket and we take a seat. He starts to pull out containers of food. One after another and I stare wide eyed at everything he packed. He sees my expression and laughs. "What? I didn't know what you were in the mood for, so I bought a little of everything?" He shrugs like it's no big deal and then I can't contain it anymore. I laugh.

As I come down from my laughing fit, I see Knox has gone tense. I look around but don't see anyone, but then I feel it. The surrounding air is filling with energy and my magic begins to feel like an excited puppy bouncing around inside my chest. When I finally pinpoint where the energy is coming from, I look behind me. Sure enough, it's a fucking portal.

I mean, I've never seen one in real life, but it is like the ones I saw in that Netflix movie about a girl who dreams and then goes to some dreamland or something.

I stand with an awe expression because it's so pretty. Its bright colored lights of pink, gold and orange chasing after each other in a wide circle. *Round and round they go. When they will stop, nobody knows.*

Knox immediately stands and steps in front of me. There is a pop of white light and I frown because I wanted to see the pretty lights. "Hey, I wanted to see that." I whisper, while tapping Knox's shoulder. But he is currently acting like a brick wall. "Excuse me, I am talking to you." I hear growls go up in front of us and then Knox widens his stance as if preparing for battle.

A second round of growls goes up and then it hits me. *My mates.* They came. I go to step around the wall when a dizzy spell hits. *Shit. Not now.* I stumble and fall to my knees as black dots start to appear in the corner of my vision. *Don't pass out, don't pass out.*

"I am giving you one warning. Let our mate go or we will kill you where you stand." Cas growls out. I can feel Knox's chest vibrating and then sense his shadows beginning to comfort me. I focus on what's around me, but my body and eyes feel so weighed down, like I'm wading through tar. I need to get to the guys. I know they can help me, but before I can say a word, my vision goes black.

EIGHT

Three fucking days and we have gotten nowhere with finding Azzie and bringing her home. Beasty rumbles in my chest. He refuses to be called anything but what Azzie named him. Grandma and Michael told us we needed to continue to keep up the pretense that nothing happened and that Azzie is simply sick, so we have been going to school but it's been so hard. It's like I have this weight on my chest that is trying to suffocate me, but I know deep down that Azzie could fix it. I think the guys feel it too, but none of us will talk about it.

Every day after school, we drive around and try to sense her in any way. Even just a glimpse of something, but every day we return empty-handed and it's starting to become unbearable.

Today starts the same as we all go about getting ready for school but not saying a single thing to one another. Azzie has been in our life for a few weeks and now that she isn't here, it's like we can't function. I think Cas and Kam are taking it the hardest. Grim was borderline obsessed with my angel and was basically the first to get close to her. Whereas Cas is beating himself up for failing at protecting her, again.

When we were at Mayor Blackwood's office the other day, we all knew that he had nothing to do with her going missing, but Cain and Kam mentioned they got a weird vibe from Blackwood's beta, James. Blackwood was shocked at first when we told him who Azzie was and that if the information ever got out, it wouldn't end well for his pack. He knows that if Hell were to fall, Hell's supernatural's would flee to the earth realm and, with Ash Valley being a supernatural town, they would migrate here. We had to remind him that Hell supernatural's thought that those who lived in the Earth's realm were beneath them and would more than likely challenge him for the territory. He then agreed that Azzie must be found and sent out scouts to search for a possible lost town's person and instructed them to report back to him or us.

They reported nothing has been found and will start to expand their search to towns farther out. I'm not holding my breath. They won't find anything there either since Mac and them still say that Azzie is not far.

I enter the kitchen and see the others either eating cereal or drinking coffee, and I realize that we have let this place go. The kitchen sink is piled high with cups, bowls, plates and takeout containers. The trashcan in the corner is overflowing onto the floor and I swear someone hid their dirty socks somewhere because I don't remember this place ever smelling this bad, but do I say anything? Nope, because I know everyone is so on edge that it would be an all-out war if I bought it up.

"Lets go." Cas growls out and turns to stomp away. I roll my eyes because he is not the only one who feels responsible for Azzie not being here. He may be our unofficial leader, but Azzie is all of our mates and we all failed to protect her. Beasty scoffs in my head. I know he is mad we lost our mate, but he is angry because we, despite our training, couldn't stop someone from taking her to who knows where.

We follow Cas out and all climb into his black SUV. No one says a thing till we hit the parking lot of Ash Valley High. "We will search the north side of town today. You should keep your eyes open and listen to everything said. If anyone mentions her name, I want to know." We nod to Cas, but no one makes a move to get out. After another minute or so, Remi opens the door and we all follow his lead.

As we hit the steps, my head is down, not quite focusing but still somewhat present, but then I snap my head up when I hear giggling in front of me. Low and behold, Bella and her puppy dogs are standing together giggling. I know they know nothing about Azzie, but knowing that they tried to humiliate her barely a week ago has my blood boiling. Lucky for Beasty and me, Cas steps to her, leans down and whispers something to her and seeing how fast the color drains from her face, is gold. Then a pang runs through my chest because Azzie should have been here to see that.

Bella, feeling like she has to save face for the rest of the school, straightens her back, glares and then turns to leave. "What did you say to her, man?" Remi asks before I can. Cas shrugs, "I found out yesterday that she has been sleeping with James, her pack beta. I threatened to tell her dad, you know, since James is a married man and all." He smirks and then continues towards our lockers. We all just stand there for a second and then Remi breaks us out of our shock by laughing out loud and follows behind Cas.

The first half of the school day drags on and it just makes me notice the absence of a campfire and warm marshmallow scent. I long to smell it again. As the bell rings for lunch, I drag my body out of my chair, grab my bag, and head to meet the guys.

We meet at my locker, not exchanging a single word, and head to the cafeteria. We grabbed our lunch and headed to the table where Mac, Ivy, and Caleb were seated. We quietly take our places around the table and start to eat, the silence filling the air. Five minutes in, Mac finally speaks up. "So where is the search today?" She looks around and then takes a bite of her burger.

"North side of town." Cas replies short and sweet. Mac nods back and takes another bite. About twenty minutes into eating my own burger, Mac, Ivy and Caleb freeze and look at each other. At first, I'm confused about what is happening, but Cain seems to understand. He stands and demands, "Where?" We all turn to him next because I have never ever heard such a tone come from him. By the looks on the other's faces, they are just as surprised.

"Where what dude? What is happening?" Remi asks, looking back and forth between Cain and my sister.

"Azzie." Ivy whispers, but it's loud enough to get all of our attention.

"Can you portal us?" Cas snaps at Caleb, who starts bobbing his head like one of those bobble head toys. "Outside now." He demands, and we all move at once, abandoning our lunch table and meals. We head for the door with all eyes on us, but nothing will stop us with this being the first genuine lead we've had in days. Once we hit the back doors, we head to the center of the clearing where I had beast out less than a week ago but what feels like years with Azzie not being here.

Once Cas is happy with the distance away from the school, he nods to Caleb, who moves to the front of our little group, then nods as if reassuring himself. He closes his eyes to focus and takes a deep breath. He nods once more, then moves his hands in a clockwise circle while mumbling something under his breath. At first I see nothing and am about to demand he hurry the fuck up, but then I see bright colorful lights start to follow the movement of his hands. After another second, the circle widens and the lights up bright with the colors of a sunset. Pinks, golds, oranges swirl around and around, faster and faster. I feel like I'm about to get dizzy when I see the lights open and a green clearing comes into view. I look at my brothers and Cas nods. "Let's go get our mate." Then he steps through, followed by Kam, Cain, Remi, and the girls. I look over at Caleb. "You better be right about this." I say but add on in my head, *we can't take anymore false hope.*

I've only ever been through one portal before when we came here from Hell, and I hated it then. I also hate it now; clenching my jaw to make sure my stomach contents stay where it belongs. But for a second there, I thought it was a losing battle. Once I get my bearings and can breathe again, I look around and at first only see the green field from a moment ago, but since I was one of the last to walk through; it takes me another second to notice the big guy standing just across from us. He is as big as Cas and has the brightest red hair I have ever seen. He widens his stance and I'm confused because Caleb was supposed to take us to Azzie, not some dude having a picnic in the middle of nowhere.

I hear it then. The whisper of a female's voice. "Hey, I wanted to see that." I'm once again confused for a moment because I don't see anyone else around us and I know it wasn't Mac's or Ivy's voice that I heard. Then I hear it. "Excuse me, I'm talking to you." Growls erupt around the field because that voice belongs to the one and only Azzie. My mate and Hell be damned if I let this guy take her away from me again. Beasty ripples under my skin, but I know now is not the time. *Just a little longer.*

I see Azzie take a step to move to the dead man's side when in the next second she is stumbling to the ground and lands on her hands and knees.

"I am giving you one warning. Let our mate go or we will kill you where you stand." Cas growls out, followed by the rest of us. This brute must have a death wish because he bends down and picks Azzie up, holding her carefully. Then his once dark eyes flash red and shadows start to fill the space where they just were. *Motherfucker.* Unlike last time, we don't lose her scent or energy signature, so we start the hunt. Kam and Cain shift first because they have the most sensitive noses. They sniff the air, then take off in search of our treasure. *Ready or not, here we come.*

It takes about ten minutes, but the moment the thick tree thin, my body immediately knows we found her. Cas is next to shift, knowing that we would die to protect our queen and mate. Beasty urges me to shift next and I finally give in the second my foot hits the path that leads to the front door of a cabin. Beasty roars to make our presence known. We can smell her now, but she doesn't smell right. Something is wrong, and it fuels the rage that now pumps through my veins. My mate needs me, needs us, and we are about to burn the world down to get to her.

NINE

REMI

O nce the trees thin out, we see a medium-sized log cabin and my magic sparks up. She's here. Purple and gold swirl around my vision and the need to get to her almost becomes unbearable. Who knew guys like us would fall into what I can only describe as love, with a girl that refused to talk to us for a week. Stubborn woman, but the last few days have been hell. My magic, which is usually as laid back as me, has been lashing out.

That day in the mayor's office was not just my doing. No, I heard Bella's words, but it was like my magic felt verbally attacked by them as well. I suppose it is somewhat true. Since Azzie marked us, my magic has been crawling under my skin. Which in bizarre because I don't have a shifted form but it almost feels like something wanted out. The second that Bella spoke Azzie's name; magic shot out of me intending to harm or kill her, but we pulled back before we got that far. An image of Azzie standing above Bella with a wicked grin, full of bad intentions, made me release her. *My magic was right. Azzie should be the one to destroy her.* It's only fair for what she's put Azzie through since she came to Ash Valley.

I eye the cabin and try to focus on where Azzie could be, or the asshole who thought he could take her away from me again. *Over my dead body, fucker.* I sense magic around the perimeter and focus harder. I sense two beings. One must be Azzie and the other energy must be the assholes. I take a step forward, about to charge the place, when Cas, speaking in my head, halts me.

"Wait! No one moves. Something isn't right. Why did he come back here knowing we would find them?" *Good question.* He must have known we would give chase and hunt him. So why back here?

"Azzie isn't well. Something is wrong. Her scent isn't right." Max states next, and a chill runs down my back. We haven't felt anything from her. She can't be dying, unless magic is blocking some type of wound. No. We just got her. We won't lose her.

"What are we waiting for, then?" I respond because we are wasting time standing here chit chatting.

"He is aware that he is surrounded. He has no choice but to come out and fight. I don't sense anyone but the two of them. When he comes out, Remi, we need you to go locate Azzie and bring her back to us. Got it." Cas side eyes me and I nod.

Find Azzie, bring her to safety, then destroy the ass who thought he could take our mate. Easy enough.

We don't have to wait very long. The walking dead man opens the cabin door, looks behind his shoulder, then back at us. He steps forward onto the porch and then raises his hand almost like he is surrendering, but what kind of idiot would surrender to men who look about ready to burn down the world, regardless? He opens his month to say something, but before any words can come out, chaos reigns.

All at once, Max roars, deafening my ears for a second. Kam and Cain charge behind Cas, who has shifted full demon. A rare site to see. The asshole must have thought this would happen because thick black shadow smoke like before fills the area the guys just charged. It's so thick that it even covers Beasty. This guy must be powerful to be able to control this much shadow.

I look around and realize now is my chance to move. We decided to leave the girls and Caleb on the field in case something happens, they can get Michael for backup. In hindsight, having someone who also controlled Shadowland magic might have been helpful. Too late now.

I move along the edge of the cluster fuck of darkness that's happening in the middle and make my way as quietly as possible. Not wanting to alert anyone about what my job is. *Nothing to see here. Do-do-do.* I make it to the porch and the first step creaks. *Fuck.* I freeze, but I think the growls coming from behind me are too loud for supernatural hearing to focus on my loud stepping. I move forward with my finger guns at the ready. I'm a secret spy agent and my mission is to save the hot as fuck woman from the evil mastermind who wants to destroy the world with his freeze ray.

Shit. Focus Remi. Azzie needs us.

I make it to the doorway and look behind my shoulder to check the massacre that I'm sure the guys are creating with this guy's body, but what I see makes my heart skip a beat and not the giddy, happy-go-lucky kind. Nope. The scary shadow fucker is standing at the end of the stairs with his fire red eyes peering at me like he wants to burn me alive. *Can Shadowland beings do that?* I tense for an attack because why wouldn't he? But he stands there almost as confused as me. I peek behind him and the guys must be stuck in the shadows because I can hear the growls of some pissed off beasts.

"Go. She needs us." I stare at him with my jaw probably hitting the floor. Did he just say that?

He steps towards me, and I prepare to swing, but the fucker rolls his eyes. Actually, rolls his eyes at me. *What the hell is happening right now?* He steps past me and continues through the living room area and to a hallway. He stops and must realize I haven't followed because he speaks to me again. "Are you coming? I don't think she has much time." That snaps me out of my surprised state and I follow him with my magic on high alert, but it's odd. It doesn't want to attack this guy. It seems to be searching for something else. I realize what when we stop in front of a door and this dude opens it to reveal a king sized bed with my mate passed out on top of it.

I rush through the opening but stop myself short from basically tackling Azzie. I look down at her and realize that she really doesn't have much time. She looks sick. Like death bed sick. She looks pale white, like she has never seen a day in the sun. She looks like she lost some weight as well. I place my hand on her forehead to check her temperature and she seems to be freezing and burning up all at the same time. *Shit. What do I do? What do I do? Think Remi. I need Cain. He would know what this asshole did to her.*

I gently lift Azzie into my arms, and the asshole behind me speaks again. "Careful."

"This is all your fault, asshole." He looks down, and I thought for a second I almost saw guilt, but that can't be right. He kidnapped her. Took her away from her home and mates for three whole days. He doesn't give a shit about her. He probably works for the bitch of a sister Azzie has. I can't wait to interrogate him.

"I need to get to Cain, so you're going to have to release my brothers from your shadows. He will know what to do." He looks nervous for a second, as he should. My brothers will shred him to pieces once he stops playing dirty with his shadow shit. He finally nods and I walk out at a fast pace. Azzie hasn't responded yet and

I'm beyond worried. I would even take one of her epic eye rolls she always gives me right now.

We hit the porch, and I can hear my brothers cursing up a storm. They must have shifted back and seem more pissed that they were trapped by darkness now.

"Release them." I say. The asshat next to me straightens his spine and places his palms facing out next to his side. He takes a deep breath and the shadows start to shift and move towards us. Shit, I hold Azzie a little tighter. I will not let him take her, but the shadows don't even touch us. They glide toward him, up his legs and kind of just disappear into his chest. *It's cool and really creepy at the same time.* The guys realize the darkness has faded and turn as the last of the smokey substance leaves.

"What the fuck!" Cas growls.

"Azzie!" Kam yells.

Max lets a warning growl build in his chest. But like I thought, Cain curses and steps forward. He eyes the guy next to me and the asshole raises his hands to show him he means no threat. As of now. I meet Cain at the bottom of the steps and lay Azzie in front of him. He places his hand on her forehead like I did.

"Fuck. This isn't good. Get over here now, guys." Kam and Max rush over and fall to their knees. Cas, on the other hand, rushes the shadow dude and slashes his half-shifted hand across his chest. Then grabs the guy by the neck when he tries to say something in a panic tone looking down at Azzie. *Why would he care about her?* I look back down at Azzie as my brothers continue to watch Cas whisper what I can only guess are ways he plans to kill him. When I spot blood starting to pool on Azzie chest. *What the?*

"Cain." He doesn't seem to hear me. Shit. Panic is starting to cease in my chest. *What is happening? There wasn't blood before.*

"Cain." I say louder. *Am I whispering or something?* "Cain!" His eyes snap to my face, but I can't stop myself from looking at the blood. His gaze dropped to Azzie and his eyes widened, recognizing my alarm. He looks up at Cas and the other guy and then back down. He does it several times and I finally snap.

"Cain! Fix her!" He shakes his head and mumbles something about how it isn't supposed to be possible.

Max and Kam finally seem to notice what has me in a panic because I hear Grim whine and I feel Max become a statue to my left. Cain looks behind me, and something makes me look as well. Cas is about to take another swing and then it clicks. *Fuck.*

"NOOOO!" Cain screams and stands as if to tackle Cas but my panic must provoke my magic because it whips out and whips around Cas, before he can swipe his clawed hand across the guy's throat, I pull him back and the shadow guy slumps to the floor grasping for air.

"What the fuck?" Cas roars at us. Furious, we took away his kill. He peers over at us from where I tossed him. I raise my hands to explain somehow, or something, but Cas freezes his movement and stares at my hands. I'm confused for half a second before I realized my hands are covered in Azzie's blood. *Oh Hell.* This is not a good way to calm a pissed off demon down. He stands and stalks towards us before peering at Azzie's lifeless body. He falls to his knees by her head and cups her cheek with the gentlest of touches I've ever seen him make.

"I'm so sorry, Azzie. We need you. Come back to me. I need you. I'm sorry. Please, baby girl." He whispers to her, but we can hear it all as clear as day and it rips my heart from my chest to hear him so broken right now.

There has to be a way. I look away, about to ask Cain, but he is helping the asshole up from the ground but is looking at his arm in confusion. He then moves his shirt to the side of the shred marks and then I see it. *Holy shit on a stick. That's not possible.*

Cain nods over to Azzie, and the asshat nods his head. Then they turn and walk our way. No one else notices until he is kneeling at her feet, about to place his hand on her. Cas, Kam and Max all growl, but he doesn't flinch, just pauses right above her ankle.

"We need him. He is a guardsman like us. Azzie claimed him."

"Bullshit. That can't be." Max glares at the guy, but Kam seems to be thinking. He looks from his chest to Azzie's and then sucks in a deep breath.

"Holy shit he is." The asshat turns his arm and shows us the small mark that we all hold but with six stars above the moon. Wait, ours had five. I look down and yup. I now have six stars on my mark. *Well, damn. Guess we can't kill him.*

"We have wasted enough time. She needs us. I will explain every-thing later." The guy says and then places his hand on her skin.

"Each of us needs to touch her somewhere. She needs to know we are all here with her." Cain says, while kneeling and placing his hand on her other ankle. Kam grabs her right wrist and Max grabs her left. Cas places his hand back on her cheeks. Well, shit, where does that leave me? I notice a sliver of skin at the bottom of the sweatshirt she is wearing and decide to go for it. Punch to the face by her or not. I just need her to wake up. I place my hand under her shirt and lay it flat on her belly.

Warmth fills my chest and I then I sense it. Sense her where my heart is supposed to be. An image of a moon with six stars surrounding it flashes through my mind. Azzie and her mates. Shit, I have to step up my game. Now I have five others dudes to complete with for attention.

I didn't notice my eyes were closed until I hear the harsh intake of breath, but it's not the noise that makes me focus. No, it's who it came from. Azzie.

TEN

AZZIE

U gh. I feel like a mac truck hit me, backed up and ran me over
again. My whole body hurts. Inside, outside, even my hair
hurts. I try to move to yell out for help, but I can't budge a single
muscle. It's like I'm frozen in time and a black abyss is swallowing
me whole. Pain, darkness, loneliness. I scream at the top of my lungs,
but I know I'm only screaming in my head. Then the pain crosses
my chest and a tear falls. *What is happening to me? Did my sister get
me? Why aren't my guys saving me?*

Then I hear it. A woman's voice, sweet, kind, calling for me, calling
me home. Is this the afterlife? An image of myself holding a baby
flashes in my mind, but that's not right. I look older, but not like
myself. Is my magic trying to tell me something?

Suddenly, a woman is standing next to me and I realize it's not me,
but someone who looks like me. She is beautiful. With the same light
gray eyes and the same dark hair that fades to a bright color. Hers
is a pretty shade of ocean blue and mine is the blood red color. We
both have the same facial feature but she is ageless it seems. She smiles
softly and reaches up to touch my cheek. I should flinch, but I'm
frozen still. Even if I weren't, this woman calms me. It's the strangest

feeling, like I know her somehow. A tear falls from her cheek and I'm sad with her, but why?

"My sweet little girl. It breaks my heart that I was unable to protect you from this world. I would change places with you in a heartbeat if fate would allow it, but she saw it fit you learn life is harsh to the best of us. I wish I could tell you it got easier, my dear, but the battle ahead will test you beyond your limits. Time is of the essence, but you must learn to balance the two sides of yourself. The dark and the light for Hell depends on it. Trust your men. Your sister will not play fair, but you are not just the queen of Hell, my love. Know you were always meant to be so much more." She looks behind her and when she turns back, her eyes are widened with fear. "I must go, but we will meet again, my little queen. Now you must go to your men. They need you as much as you need them. Tell your father it is time you know the truth." She leans in and kisses my forehead. She takes one more look at me as more tears fall from her rosy cheeks and fade into the dark abyss around me. That's when I feel the warmth spread through all of my body.

My eyes snap open to the brightest light ever, blinding me as I gulp in air like I am a fish out of water. Honestly, after what I just saw, I feel like one. *Where the hell am I and what the hell happened to me?* My body still aches like I got ran over, but the pain is calming with the warmth coming from around me. That's when I hear the voices all around me, bombarding me with questions. It's so loud that I wince and whoever is at my head growls. That must be Cas. I tilt my head up to check and the look I see on his unnaturally good-looking face suddenly worries me. "What's wrong?" I ask. I don't like this look on his face. It doesn't fit. He starts laughing then and I get even more confused.

He leans down and whispers, "Only you would be worried about someone else at a time like this?" I furrow my brow because a time like what? Then while I try to remember what happened, Cas leans further over me, grabs my cheeks and kisses me. *Holy shit, Cas is kissing me.*

You know that scene in Spider-man when he is hanging upside down and he kisses Mary-Jane? Yeah, I totally got butterflies from this kiss. Holy shit! My first kiss ever and it's with Cas, of all people. *Did I die or something?*

"Close but no. You didn't die. You did give us one hell of a scare." He pops his head up a little right as I jerk up in surprise and our foreheads collide. "Ouch."

"Careful, my queen." Knox says and I turn around, still in shock because I could have sworn Cas spoke in my head. But how? I know it's possible, but we didn't bond, so it shouldn't be possible. What the hell did my magic do while I was in that dark place?

Suddenly Kam is in front of me. "Breathe, Angel, breathe." I take a deep breath, but I'm still so confused. What happened? I try to think but my brain has decided playing a rock concert is more important than me getting answers.

"She will be confused for a bit. She just needs to rest, but let's get her back to the warehouse so we can figure some things out. This just got more complicated." I mentally roll my eyes, but even that hurts.

Stupid Cain and his smart, sexy brain always being right, but I need coffee, not rest. I also need to talk to Michael.

"We can get you coffee to sweetheart." Max says and now I think I'm going crazy again. *Are they reading my thoughts or am I saying this stuff out loud?*

Remi speaks next, and for once, I'm grateful he put me out of my momentary insanity. "Azzie, not to freak you out, but like we can hear your thoughts. I'm sure Cain can explain more once we get you coffee. So, keep your dirty thoughts PG, unless they're of me, of course." So, maybe Remi wasn't so helpful because the second he said dirty thoughts, my oh so unhelpful magic flashes me an image of my guys naked and me on a bed. I hear groans going up around me, and that only makes my thoughts worse. My cheeks, I'm sure, are as red as tomatoes and the wetness pooling between my legs is a welcome feeling but I'm embarrassed none the less.

Thankful someone has their head on right because I hear an ouch from Remi and a knock it off from Max. "I think its time to go. Azzie, you're still healing so someone will need to carr-," before he can finish his sentence, I'm lifted by none other than Cas, my growly demon. I can't bring myself to look him in the eyes, not after he heard my thoughts. We walk away from the cabin when he decides to break the tension building between us.

"Never again, baby girl, I promise. I will give my last breath before I let anything happen to you again. You also have a lot of explaining to do about another mate." I flush again because I swear my magic fluffs up like a damn hussy. "Rest baby. You're safe." Hearing those words must have done something to me because one moment I am inhaling Cas sandalwood and amber scent and the next my eyes are feeling heavy. This time I don't fade to that dark abyss. No, I stay warm and cozy cradled in my demon's arms.

When I wake up next, I'm snuggled between two bodies, trying to burn me alive. Holy shit, I'm sweating balls. My body now aches like I just worked out too hard instead of having a head on collision and the rock concert must have ended because now it's just fuzzy static in my head. I lean up just a little and realize why it feels like an inferno in here. Two hellhounds lay on either side of me, softly snoring and I wish I had a camera because it's the cutest thing ever. Picture perfect.

A faint chuckle reaches my ears and I turn my head towards the end of the bed where Remi is resting with his hands behind his head. "I wouldn't tell them they are cute. Hellhounds like being strong and tough and are very prideful at time." I roll my eyes. Grim and Reaper would let me call them whatever I wanted. Then I realized I didn't say that out loud.

"Stay out of my head." Remi shrugs, then turns towards me. "Don't think so loud and I wouldn't be able to hear you." How the hell do you think quietly in your own head? Remi, being who he is, starts laughing like I just told the funniest joke ever, and then I get it. "Asshole." I roll my eyes but smile. I'm glad someone can make me laugh right now because I know I have to talk to Michael after what that woman said. Maybe she was a guardian angel, but I think I know the truth and I'm not sure how to feel.

"What are you doing at the end of the bed?" I ask, not that I mind, really. Remi turns back to me and pouts. Full on lip sticking out and the worst puppy dog eyes I've ever seen, but still he makes it look adorable. "I lost rock, paper, scissors, and couldn't sleep next to you. So, I chose the end of the bed, anyway." I stare at him, a little stunned by his words, but then it was my turn to bust out laughing. I can't help it. He has to be joking, right?

My hellhounds stir at my very un-ladylike laugh, but he just said the guys played an elementary school game to choose who would sleep next to me. This is great. Not only do I have six insanely good-looking guardsmen and mates, but they choose kids' games to pick who gets to be next to me. What's next? Tic-tac-toe? Eee-nie-meenie-miney-mo? Who draws the shortest straw? I'm laughing so hard at this point that tears are falling and my sides hurt again.

"I don't think it's that funny." Remi says and I pause but he is still pouting and I break out in laughter again, but of course my good feeling couldn't last forever.

The bedroom door opens and standing there in the doorway is Michael. Before he can get any words out, I climb off the bed and rush into his open arms, breathing in his familiar scent. *Home.*

Eleven

AZZIE

"My little star. I've missed you. You gave all of us a scare. Are you alright?" He grabs my shoulder and leans me back to give me a once over. My look must assure him I'm okay, because he nods and pulls me to his chest again, squeezing the air out of my lungs.

I take a deep breath, needing to ask him about the woman in my dreams. I think I know who she is, but it's such a foreign concept that I have a mother when I was told my whole life that she was dead. "Michael, a woman who looks similar to me, came to me in a dream or something." I try to keep my voice strong and appear sure of myself, but I don't think that's how it comes out. I feel Michael stiffen under me and get the idea he knows who I'm talking about. "Sh-she told me to tell you that it was time I knew the whole truth of who I'm meant to be. What did she mean? Was she my mother?" I whisper the last part, trying to hold back the tears of losing someone that I never knew in a dream, but for that minute in time, I felt like I had known her my whole life. Her warmth filled me with what I imagine a mother's love would feel like.

I feel a wet drip fall on my cheek and reach up to wipe my eyes, but then feel another land on my forehead and I'm no scientist, but tears don't fall upwards. I peek up and realize that while yes, my eyes are leaking water, Michael's have leaked as well. That's when I know. *She was my mother.*

I grab my father tighter. Afraid that he will drift away like she did at any moment. I always joke that I wish this was a dream, but I can't imagine not having my father or even my men near now. I need to let them all know how I feel about them, but for now, I need my dad. His embrace turns just as tight almost on the side of not being able to breathe again, but I don't care. I need to find assurance that I'm not alone this time. I have this tendency to act like I don't need anyone and that I can take care of myself. However, the presence of my dad, these men, and my new friends has shown me a whole new world. *Literally, if we're counting the fact that I now live in a world full of supernatural's that I'm supposed to rule over.*

After a few minutes, Michael leans back and stares at me. "You have her eyes, you know. The lightest shade of gray, that at times almost look white. You also have her heart. She was an amazing queen. Just and fair, but she had the biggest heart I've ever seen. Much like you. This world threw you around and tried to break you down at every turn, but you still kept your heart. You have always tried to protect those who could not protect themselves, but your mother is right. I was not done telling you everything before your shadow mate decided to take you away." His smile softens, then looks over my should and smirks. I look back and all six of my mates are standing there and my shadow mate wears a guilty look upon his face. I giggle.

"I don't think you guys would have let him come up to us and introduce himself as my mate as well. He did what he thought was necessary at the time." When Knox's guilty look turns to what appears to be pride, I decide to stir the pot. "Though you did inject me with something to make me sleep and then told me I couldn't see my other mates for a few days. Which in turn started making me sick and then lead to that huge fight and me almost dying, I think." I put my finger to my chin and tap as if I'm trying to remember more, but then I hear growls and then the sound of skin hitting skin, which causes the air to leave my lungs as a hunch over in pain.

"Oh, shit. Cas, you idiot, look what you did." I feel four bodies practically push Michael out of the way and I know in my bones Max, Remi, Cain, and Kam are surrounding me. Everywhere they touch, that warm tingly feeling fills me with a soothing warmth as the pain subsides. I look up and glare at Cas, but then the look of pure horror reflects back at me. I drop my glare, but the pain I see in Cas's eyes doesn't dissipate. Reluctantly, I break free from the guys and walk towards Cas. I reach for him, but he pulls away. He must see the flash of hurt cross my face because then he rushes me and slams me against his chest.

"I'm so sorry, baby girl. Please forgive me. I keep fucking up." He whispers in my ear, almost like he thinks I will lash out at him and push him away. It's weird now that I think about it, this side of Cas that I've never seen before. Gentle, caring, we have always had a love hate relationship, but this Cas, I'm not sure what to do with.

"Stop beating up the others. He told me Frank knows where I'm at. He was doing what he thought was right to protect me. Can you say you wouldn't have done the same in his position?" I look into his eyes then and I see it when he realizes I'm right.

Of course, I'm right, but I'll choose the high road and won't brag about it.

He nods his head and smirks, then leans into whisper, "Baby girl, your pay for that comment." At first I'm confused, but then the lightbulb goes off in my head. *Damn it all to hell.*

"Stay out of my damn head!" I go to turn around, but he holds tight, then kisses me breathless. I melt into a puddle right there where I stand. Then the tables turn.

"Holy shit. I'm actually kissing her. She smells so damn good. The things I would do to her body. I would worship her at the alter because God damn that ass." Heat pools between my legs and my heart skips a beat in anticipation of said worship but I must not be the only one who heard his thoughts because Remi speaks in the next second and it's like ice cold water being splashed over my head.

"Well, hot damn. Where is this altar and when can I worship her?" I can't help it. I burst out laughing.

"Okay, this is weird guys and my dad is right there. We have more pressing matters to attend to, but we do need to have a conversation about all this." I circle my finger in a circle to in case the seven of us. That will be a whole headache in and of itself, and I really don't think I'm ready for it, regardless of what my magic may think.

I look over at my dad, and he is smiling from eye to eye. At first I think he is about to tease me, but a tear falls from his left eye and I'm about to freak out because what now? But he holds up his hands and then wipes the loose water droplet away. "Don't mind me, sweetheart. That's just the first time you ever called me dad so casually and out loud." I smile up at him. He shakes his head and then goes into a serious mode next. " I know you all just got Azzie back, and that Knox has some explaining to do, but I think Azzie needs to know the rest of her origins before anymore unexcepted things can happen." All my guys nod and start to turn to leave the room. I'm about to follow when Cas stops me.

"Azzie, can we talk tonight? I think it's time we all clear the air between us all." He says.

"Even Knox." Cas clenches his jaw and grinds out, "Yes, even your shadow mate." I give him a bright smile, teeth and all.

"Give him a chance. He is a good guy, Cas. Plus, if you hurt him, you hurt me. Remember." I smile even wider when he flexes his fist, remembering what happened a few minutes ago. To soothe the beast that I know I'm pressing buttons on, I reach up onto my tiptoes and kiss him gently on the lips. When I pull away, I see the flare of heat in his eyes and take off after the others before anything comes of this kiss. As I cross the doorway, I hear him growl out, "You're playing with fire, baby girl." But all the growl does is send more heat to my already burning core and butterflies to my belly.

Walking into the living room washes away the butterflies that filled my stomach a few seconds ago. The realization that there are still things about myself that others know and I don't.

How much worse can this information really get?

The moment that thought crossed my mind; I knew I screwed up. *Why would I think it couldn't get worse? It can always get worse.* My whole life has been one tragic story after another, with a few epic sprinkles of what the fuck just happened and a whole lot of just keep on moving. But as I think all this, can you get much worse than a sister who wants to kill you and six men that you have to balance and hope don't kill each other or me in the process? *Yeah, it totally can't get much worse. Said no reasonable person ever.*

My mind must have been broadcasting to all my men because when someone says my name and I look up and six of them are staring at me in a wide range of emotions. Worry being the most common but I see a bit of anger there, as well. *Great, does this mind link shit have an off switch, or maybe a mute button?*

I release a heavy sigh. "Everything is alright. I promise. Just a lot has happened and I haven't had time to digest it all. So, give me a break. After this conversation, I should be all caught up, right?" I see a few nods and a few side eyes at each other and now I have a sinking feeling everything is about to get worse.

I head over to where my dad sits, and he pats the seat next to him on the couch and, like children, my guys rush to be the one that sits on my other side. I roll my eyes. "Do boys ever grow up?" I ask my dad, but he shakes his head and laughs. "Nope, me and your mother's other men were the same way. We always wanted to be near her. To comfort, to make her smile or laugh, or to just hold her hand. She was the sun to our sky and the brightest thing you could see in a room. Her smile could stop time, I swear, and the moment it was focused on you, there wasn't a single thing she could say that you wouldn't do." He smiles as if remembering her. I wonder how long it's been since they have seen each other? Three days away from my men and I felt horrible. How can they be away from each other like this? I'm about to ask when he continues to speak.

"Little Star, this bond that you have with them is not a curse. Some days it may feel overwhelming and other days I'm sure you will want to kill them all, but you are a gift to them and I promise you, there is not a single one of them that is not head of heels for you. It's not just the magic, either. Fate created you all to be as one. Think of it as a heart. They are the six pieces that make up your heart and you are the glue and strength that keeps it beating and together. One piece of you is a part of them and vice versa. Just remember that when the time comes." He looks over to Birdy and she winks at me. Damn seers and dad's being vague and mysterious.

I'm about to demand that they tell me what the hell they know, because I feel like I only ever know bits and pieces, but yet, I'm supposed to save Hell. *How do you save something with no information?*

"Azzie!" I hear and I whip around to see my three favorite people enter the doorway from the kitchen. I get up and rush to them, meeting them halfway with open arms. We end up in a big awkward group hug, but it's perfect. "We missed you." Mac breathes out into my ear.

"I missed you guys too!" I replied, my hold becoming stronger. I never imagined I'd find people who could make me feel like I'm at home, but each and every person in this room has made me believe it can be a reality.

"Ummm, Azzie. I know we joked about harems and all, but who the hell is the tall, redheaded hunk and can I call dibs?" Caleb says in a purr. Nope. My magic raises to the surface, ready to defend what is ours.

"Mine." I practically growl out, startling myself and my friends. I cover my mouth in shock, unable to believe what I had done, until I hear laughter coming from behind me. At the sound, I snap my head around and see all six of my guys are in hysterics, like I had just delivered the best punchline ever. I glare at them. "This isn't funny." I say, but have no actual anger behind my words. When I turn back to my friends, I see them trying to hold back their own laughs as well. I throw my hands in the air and head back to my spot on the couch between Michael and Kam. The moment my back is turned, my so-called friends start laughing as well.

I roll my eyes as I take my seat and hear Remi in my head. "That was hot. Possessive of us already, I see, little rebel." I sharpen my glare on him, but he smirks and I can't keep my glare much longer. So, I turn back to my dad.

"So, what more did I need to learn about myself that you should have told me years ago?" I see him wince from either my bitter tone or from my statement. Not sure which one. "Sorry, I didn't mean it that way." I look down at my hands. He reaches over and grabs one in his, squeezing in reassurance.

"Yes, you did, and you are right. I was afraid what would happen if you knew too soon but you have a right to know everything but Little star, you won't want to hear some of it. It may be more overwhelming than you think, but you need to know the whole truth." He says and as I look up and see that he is just as nervous to tell me as I am to hear it, a pit starts to form in my stomach.

I should have known it could get worse.

TWELVE

KNOX

"**M**ine." My head snaps over to my queen because I almost can't believe what she just growled out. Growled.

I heard her guy friend joke about calling dibs on me but the second she said that word claiming me and the others, my chest filled with pride and my shadows urge me to reach out and show her what belongs to her but I stop myself. *Now is not the time to woe my mate.* No, I look over at her dad and tilt my head. He looks so familiar but I can't place from where.

The incubus mix voice, if I remember correctly, Remi, fills my head. "That was hot. Possessive of us already, I see, little rebel." He purrs and Azzie glares over at him, but he smirks until she looks away and back to her dad.

"So, what more did I need to learn about myself that you should have told me years ago?" I see him wince from her tone, but I'm not surprised by it. She had a right to know about her history and who she is. "Sorry, I didn't mean it that way." She looks down, but he reaches over and grabs her hand in his.

"Yes, you did, and you are right. I was afraid what would happen if you knew too soon but you have a right to know everything but little star, you won't want to hear some of it. It may be more overwhelming than you think, but you need to know the whole truth." He says to her and I can feel the dread coming off of her in waves of anticipation for what he is about to say.

Before he can start, I have to know how I know him. So, before I lose my nerve, I blurt it out. "I know you from somewhere. Don't I?" Azzie looks back and forth between us, brow furrowed in confusion. He slowly nods his head, looking around the room before taking a deep breath.

"My younger brother was King Morningstar, when I stepped away, and your father was one of my best friends growing up. I was there when you were born, young prince Knox." Then, like a shock to my system, I remember him.

"King Morningstar. It was said you died of natural causes. What happened?" Then the lightbulb goes off. *Holy shit.* I look back and forth between him and Azzie. He sighs but nods in agreement to my unspoken question, while Azzie continues to look confused.

"This is not how I wanted to tell her." He says after a minute. Azzie furrow deepens.

I'm still in a bit of a shock that I don't process his words and rush out my own in excitement. "My queen. Why didn't you tell me? This makes so much more sense now. You acted so unsure of me and my shadows, but you were just guarding your own. Makes sense, since you didn't know if I was working for your sister or not. I'm not to clarify but this is amazing. You are the first of your kind and can unite both the Shadowland and the Royal Lands. After you found out who I was, why didn't you tell me then?" As I look up at her, I expect to see happiness or excitement, but I see horror, shock, fear. *What did I do?* Then the words Michael spoke before my rant finally connect and I realize what I've done. *Fuck.*

"Way to go, asshole. I think you broke her." The dragon, Max says in a dark tone.

I'm frozen in fear. *Will she reject me now that she knows? Why did I open my mouth to begin with?*

"Little star?" No answer. "Sweetheart?" Still no answer. "Azzie!" Finally she snaps her head to her father. He opens his arms, and she leans into him. My fear of rejections skyrockets. She hasn't even spared me a glance while the other men keep looking back and forth, waiting for something to be said. Cas with a smirk like he enjoys the grave I just dug myself.

I hear a muffled noise like Azzie is trying to speak but she is still embraced by her dad, when he leans back, I think she is crying and I'm about to go to my knees and beg for forgiveness, anything to prevent her from sending me away. From breaking our bond, but what she does surprises not only me but wipes the smirk right off that smug demon's face. She laughs. Not a sweet that's funny kind of laugh. No, she is full on belly laughing with tears in her eyes.

Did I actually break her? Like has so much been thrown at her that her mind can't comprehend what I just said. Did she not understand that she is of shadow blood as well? Not just any shadow blood, the original shadow royal bloodline. She is of two powerful bloodlines, which means she is beyond any of us can imagine. I look up at Michael, my eyes wide in shock. Do the others know the whole truth? They didn't react to finding out about her being part shadow kind, but do they truly understand?

THIRTEEN

AZZIE

I jinxed it. I knew I did the second I said it couldn't get worse, but now I'm part shadow being. The thing that everyone I know is afraid of or hates. I can't even bring myself to look at anyone. Afraid of the fear or worse, disgust I will see from my guys. They must be in as much shock as me if the only sound in the room is my hysterical laugh that I can't seem to control.

When Knox started his excited rant about me being like him and how happy he was had confused me. Of course I was like him. I'm a supernatural according to everyone, but the only magic I seem to possess is a horny whip like thing that likes to collect men as mates like we are collecting trading cards. As he continued to speak, what he was saying finally sank in that he was talking about his shadows and that I had some too, but then he brought up me uniting both the lands and that's when I think I lost it.

When I finally calm down enough to talk, I tick off my list of things I've learned and now are excepted to do. "So, let me get this straight. I'm the rightful queen of Hell, whose sister wants to kill her for a power that she can't even have. I have to prevent her from destroying Hell and making earth basically the new Hell. I have six men that I have to bond with, that probably got forced into this by my crazy horny magic that seems to collect men for fun. You all probably also hate me now since you know apparently I'm a freak everywhere I go and I'm not just a Royal Land but also a Shadowland, which means now I also have to unite both lands. Is that all?" I throw my hands up in the air, but drop them again. I'm still looking down, not risking the looks that could break me, but someone places a finger under my chin and lifts. Kam. My sweet and quiet hellhound is now kneeling in front of me, but I'm shocked when there is no disgust in his gaze.

Then I noticed the guys were surrounding me. Cain to my left, Cas to my right, and Max and Remi kneel on either side of Kam. All placing a hand on my body in a light caress that made warmth slowly spread. I look at each of them, excepting something. Some kind of disgust or anger or even fear, but I see none of it. "Angel, your father told us when you were taken what your true origins were and we have accepted you for what you are. Plus, it seems fate made that decision for us as well." He looks behind him where Knox sits looking over at me in guilt, but why? "We knew you were going to be special. We just never knew you would be this special. You are a miracle in and of itself, and we are honored to be apart of this with you." Kam rubs his palm across my cheek and then uses his thumb to wipe what I'm guessing is another stupid tear escaping without permission.

Knox stands and comes near. When he reaches us, he kneels and bows his head. "Please forgive me Azzie. I did not know you weren't aware of this. It was wrong of me to make the assumption you had, but I won't apologize for being delighted that there is a stronger relationship between us now. I did not understand why fate would mate our two kinds, as it has never been done to my knowledge, but it seems your father may need to explain a bit more about what this really means to all of us." He says, then lifts his head and I see the guilt fade as I smile at him. I look towards my father, who is already looking at us with a small smile as well. He nods.

"Yes, there is a bit more you must know, and I will ask that your men stay near you as I speak. Please understand, your mother had no idea who you would become and the power that you would possess when you were born. Fate tells no one her actual plans, just bits and piece." I nod slowly, unsure if I can really handle anymore crazy life changing news, but then Remi has to open his big fat mouth.

"It can't really be that bad, can it? We already know she is powerful, and that she is both Royal and Shadow. Ouch, fucker." He says, and I see Max pulling his arm away from hitting Remi on the back of the head. I groan.

This is about to get so much worse.

Before we could get into anything Birdy interrupts, I had almost forgotten that my friends and her were still in the room. She told us we need a lunch break, and that she made some sandwiches and put out some odds and ends in the kitchen. When I go to get up, Cain stops me. "One of the guys will bring you something. Just sit." I nod, but as the guys get up one by one, the warmth I was feeling fades. *Is the warm and fuzzy feeling that keeps happening coming from the guys?* It's like every time one or all touches my skin, it tingles as a warm and content feeling clouds my mind, but I still allowing me to focus. It's almost like the feeling I got when I was in the dark abyss and my mother showed up.

My magic that had been oddly quiet for a while peeks up in my chest and tugs me against Cain, he sucks in a breath and I don't blame him because I didn't mean to basically climb into his lap but as I try to climb off and apologize for it he grips my hips and growls his disapproval. *Okay, then.*

"Stay." Then after a second, "Please." I nod because I actually didn't want to get off. He is nice and toasty, probably because of being a hellhound. My magic, that little minx, sends me a mental wink and calms back down into my chest. Almost like being near our mates calms us somehow. I really need to figure out how to control her and her urges, but this isn't bad as long as we don't collect anymore.

Within minutes, Max is handing over a roast beef sandwich and a handful of chips on the side. "Is this okay? I can make you something else, if you want. There was turkey and ham. I should have asked you what you wanted." He goes to pull the plate away and I snatch it back, grab the sandwich and take a huge bite. I start to chew and realize I haven't eaten in who knows how long. To prove a point, my stomach makes a god-awful roar and my cheeks turn bright red in embarrassment. I never claimed to be ladylike, but I do have manners.

"Sorry. No, this is fine. Thank you, Max." I smile and it's his turn to have his cheeks turn a rosy color. I take a chip next, but pause before I take a bite, then turn to Cain and offer it to him. His eyes widen for half a second before he takes it into his mouth and chews. I smile with satisfaction.

"Thanks Kitten." I turn to face him and he shrugs. "Reaper named you, not me." I giggle at that. It feels like a weight is lifting off my chest, but then it all comes crashing back down to earth when my dad clears his throat.

"Azzie, it's best if we get this all out now. I know it's a lot, but if your mother thinks it's time to tell you all, things must be moving a lot faster than we thought in Hell." Shit, his right. My mother seemed worried before she faded away. I nod in agreement.

"Before I begin, boys, we haven't told you the whole truth either, so I need you all to keep your beast and tempers under control." He gives each of the guys a serious look but softens his eyes when they land on me. I nod again, letting him know I'm ready and Cain squeezes my hips once more before moving me to sit in the middle of the couch and the guys all take seats around me, trying to get as close as possible.

"First, I must explain a bit of history that we stopped telling over a thousand years ago. Hell is what we call our area of the realm, but it had a name before it became Hell to us. Hell was once known as the Chaos Realm. The birthplace of all supernatural kinds. The birthplace of all kinds of magic. A prophecy was given by a seer that one day a young queen would be born and she would be the rightful heir to the Chaos Realm. You see, the Shadowland and the Royal Lands were at war. So, the leaders at that time chose to close off all territories in fear that this young queen would have too much power and no one was willing to give up their thrones to have a single ruler of the realm. Silly old men, thinking fate would just agree and move along." He shakes his head and that sinking feeling I was getting now hits rock bottom. He can't be serious.

He finally takes a deep breath and continues. "Little star, it's true that you are of both Royal Land blood and Shadowland blood, but what many don't know," he looks over at Knox, who nods and now I'm getting a horrible feeling I know where this is going. "What many don't know is that Shadowland used to be ruled by one royal shadow family. This family was the original shadow kind and, at some point, decided to break up the territory into three kingdoms, but the original family has always been the strongest of bloodlines." He looks down and then looks back up and meets my eyes. "I am Michael Morningstar, from the original shadow line and you, Azzie, were born of two very powerful original bloodlines. You, my daughter, are not only the first of your kind and the queen of Hell. You are the true queen of the Chaos Realm." I stare at him, waiting for the punchline. The drum set going off when people are supposed to laugh at the joke, like at comedy clubs. Something to let me know that my life is just one big cosmic joke that fate has been telling. Anything really, but no one laughs or jumps out yelling got you or you've been punked.

My brain is in overdrive and just can't think straight to respond. So, I just sit there, wondering if all those nights I wish my life was different were all being saved for this one moment. *Fuck my life!*

Fourteen

CAS

Well, shit.

No one moves or says a thing. Probably in fear of startling Azzie in her state of shock? Speechlessness? Or the fact that what we know as Hell is actually just a smaller part of a bigger realm called the Chaos realm, and Azzie is the queen of it all. Yeah, no pressure at all.

As my mind wonders about all the possible ways this can go wrong, Remi's voice reaches out to us. "Holy shit, did any of you just realize that we have always been called the Chaos Kings and I don't even know how the name really started, but now Azzie is the actual queen of Chaos? Isn't that crazy?" Huh? He's right.

"We have bigger problems right now." I turn and glare at Azzie's asshole shadow mate. "Stay out of our heads. You may be one of her mates, but you are not a brother to us." I growl back. He rolls his eyes.

"It's not about us, demon. Do you not feel Azzie's power? It's flowing in waves almost, like something is wrong." I stop and that's when I feel it. Azzie's power is swirling and I don't think she even knows it's happening. She is in a trance of some sort. Just sitting there, staring out into space, and then I see it. The black and red swirls of her magic wrapping around her in a soft embrace. *What the fuck is going on?*

"Everyone, move away, slowly." Michael says as he stands and slowly lifts his hands.

"Why? We aren't leaving her!" Kam growls out. He's right. The six of us don't move, but I can feel the pressure building in the room.

"Yes, you are. Azzie isn't here right now. Her magic is taking over and must feel her being overwhelmed, so it's trying to protect her. You need to step away slowly." He says calmly manner but his face shows the worry that we are all starting to feel.

"Her magic knows us. It wouldn't hurt us." Remi says all confident like and goes to reach for her but, before he can touch her, magic whips out and sends him flying into the chair across the room. *Fuck. What is going through her mind right now?*

"Like I said, this isn't Azzie right now. Her mind must be trapped inside itself. I knew this was going to be too much. I understand as mates you don't want to leave her, but you need to back away now." Just as he says that, Azzie, who until now only showed a small energy burst, blasts out a wave of energy so strong that it pushes not only us but everything in the room up against the walls, pinning us there. Luckily, Birdy and the others got out before this show of power.

"What do we do now?" Cain asks, but Michael seems so surprised by the current events happening in front of us that he only mumbles out the words. Luckily, we have supernatural hearing. "I've only ever heard of this happening and never to this extent. Azzie, her mind is in what Ava calls the abyss. It's a dark place. I think that's where she was when she saw her mother. She had been there once but never told us why. Sh-she said it was painful at times. When we asked how she got out of it, she simply said she had someone to guide her and never said more."

"There has to be a way!" I growl. We have to help her if she is in pain. *Why do we keep failing her?*

"You all need to let her know you're here. Anchor her to the here and now. Boys, this won't be easy." He looks at us and we nod in understanding. Anything for our queen.

"We don't care if it's not easy. She needs us." I say back, trying to move my limbs, but her power keeps pushing down on me.

"Her magic is going to push back until Azzie can sense you. It will be painful, worse because you will feel whatever she is feeling in her mind. Whatever you do, do not force her out of the abyss. She has to return on her own or we could lose her to it. Do you understand?" His voice leaves no room for argument. I look at my brother and her shadow mate and see the determination. I nod once more and steel my spine. *Hold on baby girl, I'm coming.*

"What do we need to do?"

"Reach for your connection with her. It's weak because you have not fully bonded, but it's still there. Focus on that and send her your strength, love, and energy. She probably doesn't realize that she is even doing any of this. Focus on her. Everything you have, send her way. Reach for her mind, tell her you're here." As he is saying these words, I focus on her.

The day I first saw her in the cafeteria, sitting alone in the corner. She was breath-taking, and I only saw her from afar then, but I knew then that she was the one. I just couldn't believe it. We had waited three years, and she acted like we were nothing to her. Not a single hint of recognition. It makes sense now, but I wasn't expecting the hurt it caused me that she didn't claim us then and there.

Then everything was confirmed when I smelt her for the first time in art class. The smell of a warm campfire and the sweet scent of melted marshmallows. The perfect combo and a scent that went straight to my dick. I was so angry she ignored us that I made myself believe she wasn't the one. That she was a witch and playing tricks on us, but I couldn't get her out of my head. Every hour, every second of every day, she was there. Taking up everything.

The night she was attacked at the club and I saw her hit the ground, my world turned upside down. Then the proof on her skin that she was our queen, our mate. The one I made hate us by acting like an asshole. Scaring her when I realized she truly knew nothing of our world and since then we have been dumping information more shocking than the last on her.

No wonder her mind is fighting back. She was just told that an entire realm is hers and she has to save it from her bitch of a sister that wants her dead.

I'm sending all of my energy to her. At first I feel no change but then I can move a bit and then, as if Azzie is calling out to us, I feel a tug in my chest pulling me to her. I move without thinking. As do the others, the six of us stop mere inches from Azzie. Not exactly afraid to touch her, but we all saw what happened to Remi. I look at the other five men standing before me, knowing what we need to do. I nod in confirmation and we all slowly reach for her.

I'm confused at first, but then the pain starts and I hear the groans from the others start up as well. *Shit, is this what Azzie is feeling right now?* Before I can say or even think, the pain intensifies, and then blackness consumes me.

Fifteen

AZZIE

Pain radiates through my head, reminding me of being at another rock concert. I cry out because the pain seems to wrap around me. I peel open my eyes to see why no one is helping me, but it's dark.

The abyss.

I'm starting to really hate this place. I grab at my head as images flow through it. Images that seem familiar somehow, but none of them make sense. It's like watching a movie through someone's eyes. I see my mother, well, who I assume my mother is. She looks like the woman who visited me here before. She is holding a baby and I see my dad standing next to her with three other men. *My fathers?* They are staring in awe at the baby, and then I hear my mother whisper. "She is the one. The next true queen. She will change everything." She reaches up and grabs my father's hand and smiles. "We must protect her until her eighteenth birthday, when she takes her throne. Her powers can be transferred on that night. Someone with this kind of power could control all supernatural beings." My father nods. "We will protect her, my love. She is my little star and a queen to be, just like her mother." He strokes his palm down her cheek as a tear slips free.

Suddenly rage fills me like an inferno. My vision shifts and i have a different view. The person I am seeing through turns and stomps away down a hallway. Is this rage coming from them? Why are they so angry?

The image jumps once more and now the person I'm seeing through is talking to a man. I can only see his back, but I hear the venom coming out of me or this person. "You will take her and you will teach her nothing of our kind. Nothing. Keep her weak, scared of her own shadow. Ha. I don't care what you do to her, but you will bring her to me on the day before her eighteenth birthday. We can have a little reunion, of sorts." Then she breaks out in a laugh that sends chills rushing down my spine. I have a feeling I know who this is.

My vision jumps to another scene. I'm standing in a tower over-looking the most beautiful landscape I've ever seen. Hell. It's just as Michael told me it was, but the rage and hatred filling me ruins the warmth that the scenery just gave me. As I focus on the landscape, I realize why we are here. She wanted a front-row seat at the destruction she caused. I see the shadows moving through the town below, and then the screams begin. I try to close my eyes and cover my ears, but this is not my body right now. It's hers. One by one, the screams get closer to the castle, fires starting as homes get destroyed. Then I feel her joy, her excitement, I feel her lips lift into a smile. "Now let's go visit my dear sister. Shall will Frankie boy?" She turns and then I see him, the man from earlier. *Frank.*

The next image is different. The emotions are sad, fearful, but loving. I'm confused at first because I've been peering through my sister's eyes and feeling her emotions. The images come into focus and this person is holding a baby now. Me. If the hair and eyes are anything to go by. A tear falls onto my cheek and I realize this person is crying and that's why it's so fuzzy. "I'm so sorry, my little queen. I could not prevent this from happening. When the time is right, you will know what to do. Trust in your magic, my dear. I have little time but I have seen your future. You have not lived a simple life and fate was cruel to put you through all that, but you are a stronger being because of it. You were taught that a queen never bows and you, my dear, are the Chaos Queen. Your sister will not fight fair. She will plan to use your loved ones against you. Stay strong and do not give in to her." She runs her finger along my forehead and down my cheek and it's like I can feel her warmth in real life. "Your magic will not wait until you are eighteen. When your six come for you, embrace them. Set it free, but keep it hidden. She will underestimate you and your men and for that, she will lose it all. I must go now. She is coming to take you from us, but we meet again, my daughter. That I am sure of. Until then, I bless you with the sight." She kisses my forehead and a wave of pure bright light and energy runs through my body.

When the light clears and the warmth fades, the pain intensifies again. I grab my head and scream. I scream for what feels like hours, but that can't be. The pain comes in waves and my throat is hoarse. *I can't keep doing this.* A moment of clarity hits. I need my mates. Words whisper around me as a breeze of the wind on a chilly fall day brushes past me. "When your six come for you, embrace them." That's what she said. I call out to them.

"Caspian! Kamdon! Cain! Remi! Maxwell! Knox! Come!" My magic responds and I feel six strands of energy shoot from my chest and tug. My mates. My head builds with the pressure of the pain again. I try to fight it, just a little more energy to call to them. They're almost here. I can feel it just out of reach. As I'm about to scream out from the pain once more, warmth suddenly fills me. All around me, cocooning me in a soft and sweet embrace.

"We got you, baby girl. We are here." Cas.

"Angel, give us your pain." Kam.

"Sweetheart, listen to our voices." Cain.

"Kitten, relax." Max.

"My queen, just breathe." Knox.

"Little rebel, come back to us. I'll feed you pizza." Remi.

I want to laugh because Remi would make a poorly timed joke, but darkness overcomes me and the pain washes away as I become surrounded by my mates.

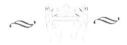

Every single damn time I pass out, I'm waking up like I've been sitting in a gods-damn sauna for hours. Sweat dripping down my body like I'm bathing in it. I want to say it's horrible and disgusting, which it is, but I also know it's because my men are surrounding me. My body aches and as I try to roll over to get more comfortable, my face hits a chest. A very naked chest. The smell of sandalwood and amber fills my nose. I would know that scent from anywhere. *Caspian.*

"Baby girl." He rasps out, his voice sending a sliver of pleasure down my back. Well, that's a first. I peek up at him through my lashes. He smirks, as if he knows exactly what he is doing to me. *Bastard.*

"How long have I been out? What happened?" As soon as I ask, my magic decides to grace me with a flashback of everything I saw while in that dark abyss place.

Before he can answer, I hold my hand up. "Never mind. I remember." He takes a deep breath and inhales my scent as he leans into me. His scent getting stronger as well. *Focus Azzie.* "I saw what happened." I whisper. Not sure why I'm being quiet. I can feel my other mates in the room, not asleep anymore, as if the moment I woke, so did they.

Cas gives me a confused look. "What do you mean, baby?" He lifts his hand and shifts my hair behind my ear in a soft caress. *Okay, who the hell is this guy?* I narrow my eyes on him. *Am I still in a dream or something?* He rolls his eyes at me. "No, this is real baby girl. I'm real." He takes my hand and places it on his chest. I feel the heat of his body and the thump thump of his heart. "I just almost lost you again." He leans in closer, his lips glazing my ear, and whispers. "Scare me like that again and I will spank your ass in front of all your mates until it's as bright as your hair and you're begging me for mercy." Then being the asshole he is, nips my ear lobe making me softly moan out.

Holy shit, that was hot. I bet my cheeks are as red as he just said. *Damn, I didn't even know dirty talk was so hot.*

"Dude. Not fair. Don't turn her on yet. We still have to talk and I'm just saying I called dibs first. Ouch, asshole. I did." Remi says from somewhere behind me and I giggle. *These men are going to be the death of me.* Cas winks down at me.

"As I was saying," I clear my throat and try to think about the visions and not my six men possibly, all half naked, lying around me ready to touch me and make me feel good. Growls go up around the room. *Shit.* "Sorry, anyway. When I was in the dark place, I had visions of the past. I was confused at first, but then I realized I was seeing through my sister's eyes. She wasn't right. I could feel her hatred she had for me. The envy and how she wanted me dead at first, until she heard my parents talking about the fake power transfer. She came up with the plan to use the shadow kind against them. I sa- I saw-" I swallow the feeling of gravel in my throat.

I'm lost in the town's vision being torn apart when an arm wraps around my middle and a chest becomes flush with my back. "Shhh, sweetheart. We know." They know? I turn slightly and see a sad look that shouldn't belong on Max's handsome face. He nods and I let out the breath that I didn't realize I was holding. I really didn't want to explain the horror I saw that night through my sister's eyes.

"I saw her." I take a deep breath, embracing the sense of safety that the guys give me. "My mother. She was whispering to me. Like she knew I would see that moment in the future." I close my eyes. Nervous about explaining or even express the next part. "She told me to embrace you all. That my powers wouldn't wait until my eighteenth birthday." I close my eyes tighter. "I need you." The intakes of breath can be heard all around me. "I need you all. Please." My body starts to heat and my magic swirls in my chest. My nerves slowly fade to excitement. I'm holding my breath at this point, excepting some sort of protest. Denial. Maybe even some sort of disgusted noise.

They know what I am offering. Once we go through with this, there is no turning back. My magic may have chosen them without my opinion and started the bonding process, but only I can choose to give them my body, my heart and my soul. If they accept, it means forever. At least that's what I've read in the various books and knowledge that Mac and the others have given me.

No one says a thing. No one even moves a muscle. My heart stops and the breath in my lungs freezes. Liquid fills the edge of my eyes.

I knew they were disgusted with the scars and the way I look. They don't want me. They don't want this. It was too good to be true to have someone want me in this way or anyway, really.

I just want to crawl into a ball and have the bed swallow me whole. Make me disappear. Anything to not be here.

Sixteen

Holy shit. Does she really want us? I look up at Cas from over Azzie's shoulder. He looks just as stunned as me. Before she was taken from us, she wanted nothing to even do with us. She wouldn't even talk to us for an entire week. It was a long torturous week, too.

No one moves a muscle; I think in fear of her changing her mind or maybe it's because at any second we are all going to jump at the chance to please her to make her ours. My heart feels like it's about to beat out of my chest. She starts to move, as if she is going to get up. "Never mind. I- I'm sorry, I asked. I'm sure my body is not the most pleas-", before she can even finish that ridiculous statement, every male in the room growls in protest.

"Don't you dare even think that, sweetheart." I say. "You are the most beautiful woman we have ever seen." She scoffs. *Of course, she doesn't believe me.*

"Do you not believe us?" Remi asks from the end of the bed. She shakes her head and I notice she still hasn't opened her eyes.

"Well, I guess we will just have to change your mind, baby girl." Cas purrs into her ear. *Have you ever heard a demon purr? It's a little creepy.* Azzie's whole-body shivers in anticipation of his statement.

Azzie takes a deep breath then, trying to relax, and I reach my hand up and shift loose hair behind her ear. Leaning forward, I kiss her neck and feel her shiver against me. I can feel my beast's excitement for what is to come as we inhale her heavenly scent. "You're about to have a very long night, baby girl. Are you ready?" Cas chuckles.

"Or we can get her ready." He runs his fingers down the other side of her face as the other four move in closer. Reaching out to touch and to caress our nervous little mate. At the exact moment all six of us are touching her, she lets out a low moan. I smile. Our connection is growing. I've noticed a few times that when all of us are near her, the energy around my little kitten shifts and grows stronger. Pulling us in as if she were a siren. Calling us to be near her at all times. *I wonder if she even realizes she is doing it.*

I lean in and kiss the side of her neck again at the same time Cas leans in to kiss her collarbone. We have never shared a woman before. We knew we would at some point, but I suppose I never thought our first time would be with her together. The intake of breath causes my beast to purr in delight. *The crazy bastard.*

I mind link the others. "How are we going to do this? This is her first time. We have to be gentle."

"I already called dibs assholes." Remi says as he slides his hands up Azzie's leg from her ankle, making goosebumps appear in its wake. He grins wide, leaning down to kiss the inside of her ankle. "I can make her feel the best."

We all scoff at that. "Just because you are part incubus does not make you some sex god. Plus, she knows you've been with Bella and her merry band of sluts." Kam growls out. "She should be with someone who has waited for her." He leans into her and takes a deep breath. Almost like he is trying to savor her scent. Me too brother, me too.

"I agree with my brother. We could ease her into all this." Cain says next, doing the same thing his twin just did. I don't blame them. Her scent is addictive, like a drug, almost.

It's the asshole Knox that speaks out loud. "My queen, how would you like this to work? We all want you, but this is your choice and we are yours to command." He adds his own little purring noise and I almost laugh.

"I- I may never have done anything like this, but I've had toys and watched porn before. I know how sex works. Now, is someone going to please me or will I need to do it myself?" Azzie says as she arches her back up off the bed as Cas runs a hand down her chest over her shirt. The silence is thick after her statement. And then Remi breaks out laughing.

"No need for that little rebel. You have six of us. We are merely asking who do you want first and who do you want where?" He replies and then leans in to kiss her thigh. More goosebumps break out across her skin and I swallow the growl of delight that we affect her so easily.

"Play rock, paper, scissors for all I care. I just need you all. Please." The moment the word please left her pretty plump lips we were goners.

Five of the six of us grew up together and worked like a well-oiled machine and having Knox with us felt like it was going to disrupt things but to my surprise he moves with us as if he has been a part of us since day one. It's odd really, but fate had plans for the seven of us and who am I to disagree with them?

Cas shifts his hand to his demon claws and rips through the shirt Azzie has on, while Cain and Remi slide down her underwear in a slow motion. Teasing her. She has yet to open her eyes and Cas notices too. He leans in and whispers to her, loud enough for us to all hear. "Open your eyes, baby girl. We want you to see what we are going to do to this beautiful body of yours. How we will not only please you, but make sure you will never want to leave this bed again. Like I said earlier, there are six of us and one of you. You are in for an endless night. So watch as we destroy this body of yours." Her eyes snap open and the inhale of breath tells me she was not excepting those words to come out of his mouth. I look back down at her body and see her bare before us. I expect her to hide herself or be uncomfortable being naked around us. Whether that be to hide her scars or hide because this is her first time, but she doesn't. If I'm being honest, it almost seems she is flaunting her body to us. Begging us to touch her more.

"Sweetheart." She looks over at me, and my heart skips a beat. Holy shit, she is beautiful. Her eyes are half-mast and unabashed lust is the only emotion I can see. "You are going to be sore tomorrow, but we will take care of you. We will always take care of you. Do you trust us?" This is important to all of us. This answer can make or break us right now. We need her to trust us to take care of her heart, body and soul. There is no going back after this. She will be ours and we will be hers in all ways possible. She nods her head.

"We need words, angel. Use your words." Kam growls out. Not harshly, but his hound is on the edge and I'm not sure how much longer he can hang on to his reigns. "Y-Yes. I understand. I trust you all." Kam doesn't wait, he drives right in the moment she finished that statement. He licks up between her legs and they both let out a long moan. Cas moves then, taking her mouth, as they duel for dominance with their tongues. Knox, Remi, and Cain are rubbing up and down her legs and opening her up for Kam to have more access.

It's not long before she is crying out her first orgasm of the night. She slumps a little, as if just that one was too much pleasure. "Oh no, no, no, baby girl. You're not done. Not even close." Cas smiles wide. In what seems like a practice routine, we all move and switch places like we have done this hundreds of times. We haven't, but with Azzie, everything seems so natural.

We do this another five times. Each of us switching places and bringing her to orgasm. Tasting her sweet juices that made you want to live between her legs and die a happy man if you suffocated. She keeps on pleading that she needs more. She needs us to fuck her, but we continue to tease, to kiss, to touch, to give her everything but what she wants. We had to wait for her for three long years. Made us almost give up hope of her. She made us go through a week of hell when she refused to talk to any of us. So what better way to get back at her than to prolong what she truly wants? *Are we petty assholes for doing this? Absolutely.*

We had already decided that Kam would be the best to be her first. He and his hound, Grim, were her first friends here and he would be the sweetest with her and she would need that at first. We aren't exactly small men and the thought of hurting Azzie, even in the namesake of pleasure, doesn't sit well with me and Beasty.

"Please, please, I need more." She whines and the sound goes straight to my dick. Prolonging her pleasure has been just as torturous on us. I can tell the guys are in just as bad of shape as me. My balls ache and my cock is weeping. Crying out to be embraced by that tight little pussy of hers. It seems the whine broke what little hold Kam had because he crawls up Azzie's body and kisses her like his life depends on it.

He leans his forehead against her and she stares at him with such hungry eyes it's breathtaking. "Alright Angel. We are each going to take you now. We will try to be as gentle as possible." Cas snorts and Remi chuckles. Kam rolls his eyes. "Most of us will try to be gentle, but our beasts want, no, they need, to claim you. I'll go slow at first, but I only have so much restraint. After this, you belong to us. Do you understand?"

"No!" she says loud enough that everyone freezes and every muscle in my body stiffens.

Is she rejecting us? Does she not want us? Did we miss our chance with her? Did she think we didn't want her because we hadn't fucked her? We wanted to prepare her. We didn't want to hurt her. Oh, Hell's Crown, she doesn't want us. Beasty is so calm and I'm so confused.

SEVENTEEN

AZZIE

I swear men are idiots! All of them. Every single one in this damn room, at least.

They truly think I want them to stop. That I'm telling them no. They are all looking down at me in disbelief, confusion, sadness, like I kicked their damn puppy or something. I roll my eyes.

"No." I say again. "You will all belong to me." Their faces flash in relief. "Now is someone going to fuck me or do I need to find someone else?" Growls echo around the room and I smile. I knew that would get them moving. Kam, who is still between my legs, kisses me again with more intensity than I ever thought was possible for a kiss. When he is done devouring my lips, I feel him settle more between my legs. I've heard rumors of your first time being painful, but I know what actual pain is, so this doesn't compare.

He slowly slides between my folds, and I tense for a second at the odd feeling. Uncomfortable, but not entirely painful. Cas leans down and whispers into my ear. "Relax baby girl. Allow the pleasure to consume you like you consume us. You still have five more of your men, all vying for another taste of you. That sweet nectar I can smell leaking between your legs." Oh Holy shit. Who knew a little dirty talk was a kink of mine? Kam, who is still frozen on top of me, feels me finally relax and slowly starts to move. And the pleasure they spoke of is instant.

A low moan escapes my lips and Kam moves in and out slowly, building another orgasm to the surface. Who knew sex could be this amazing? Remind me to thank Mac and them for their idea of a harem of men because hot damn, having six men kissing, grabbing, caressing, whispering their dirty thoughts to me is out of this realm of my imagination.

Kam moves faster, chasing his own release. At this point, I'm lost to the feeling of bliss and the warm feeling surrounding my body. When I hear him groan around me and lean in to kiss me with passion, it tips me over the cress once again. Breathing heavily in what I can only describe as a sex high, they play musical chairs once again. This time with Cain between my legs, kissing my lips, my neck and nipping my ear. *Oh god, my ear is a pleasure button too. What the heck.*

"Good to know, sweetheart." Cain says as he nips my ear again, sending shivers down my spine and tingles between my legs.

"Stay out of my head." I reply with no real heat, since you know I can hear all their dirty thoughts too and let me tell you, these boys should be attending church to cleanse their dirty mind with the things running through them, but also my core throbs at the ideas running through their naughty minds.

"I know you're getting tired, kitten, but you are doing so good." *Praise kink. Really, now.* Honestly, I don't know if it's me or my hussy magic that is enjoying all of this.

Cain lines himself up and enters me, slow and smooth. He is longer than his brother, but Kam was thicker. Ugh. He is hitting just the right spot. He moves so slowly, I can't tell if it's prolonging our pleasure or if he is trying to torture me. I wrap my legs around him and pull him in tight. His eyes widen a fraction for half a second until he realizes I what I'm trying to say and speeds up his pace.

Someone is kissing my neck and I can hear Remi in the background say how hot this looks, but I focus on my serious hellhound as another wave of pleasurable heat consumes my core. *Is it possible to die from too many orgasms? Asking for a friend, of course.*

Cain growls out his release, making me follow up at the same time. *That's it. I'm pretty sure death by orgasm is the best way to go.* He leans down and nips my nose. "Such a good girl." Then kisses my nose. *Can someone make you orgasm with words because that should not be a thing, right?*

They all flip around again and next I'm staring up at Remi for half a second, until he grabs my hips and flips us so that I'm on top of him. "I need you to ride me, Little rebel. Ride me like you own me." he smirks up at me. *Challenge accepted.*

I lean forward and grab his shaft in my little hands. *Shit, he is big.* I gulp and hear him chuckle. I shoot him a glare, then slam myself down on him in one swift motion. That smirk that was just on his face is nowhere in sight now. He seems surprised by my bold move, so I lean forward and kiss the corner of his lips. "You belong to me, Remi. I dare anyone to tell me different. Now be a good boy and please your queen." I see him shudder and inhale deeply. Ha. *I'm not the only one with kinks.* I start to circle my lower body. Knowing that he will break first as his hands tighten on my hips. It hit me then that every guy was allowing the others to have their moment with me, but still staying close. Like they couldn't bear to go too far from me. I smile at that. I know I'm not ready for multiple men at once, but I'm sure it will happen in the future.

Just like I knew he would, Remi breaks first. He snaps his eyes open, flaring with the lust I read about incubus's having. Now it's my turn to hold on as he jack hammers up into my slick heated core like his life depended on it. Good, the faster he goes the higher my climax climbs. I feel him tense beneath me, and then he reaches up and pinches my clit hard. *Oh, hell's fire.* My orgasm shots through me like a tidal wave of pure fire and I see black spots in my vision. I place my hands on his chest to steady myself while taking in lungfuls of air. *That was intense in the best way possible.*

Next up is Knox, as he grabs me from Remi and lays me back down to catch my breath on the bed. He kisses my neck and collarbone, and I focus on the feel of his lips on my skin. I feel a cool feeling wrap around me, and it's like a balm to my overheated flesh. Sighing in relief, I hear someone growl about damn shadows and someone's asshole. I shake my head and relax into my shadow lover's arms. "My queen, you are so beautiful in everything you do, but right now, you are a goddess among mere mortals." *Awwww swoon. Did he just call me a goddess?* "Are you ready for me, my queen?" I don't think I can even speak normal words at this point, so I just nod against his chest. "Good, I've waited long enough." He whispers as he moves me onto his lap, and that's when I realize he is sitting and I'm now straddling him. I love that they keep switching positions.

He lifts me and places his cock at my entrance, allowing me to slowly slide down to get used to the new size. *Geez, how many different sizes do dicks come in? I should have done research of some sort.*

I relax my muscles and move my hips, chasing another high that my body craves. He wraps his arms around my back and pulls me even closer and grinds deeper into my heat. I moan and he groans, and it's bliss all over again.

By the time we orgasm, my body is screaming at me, but I still have two men that I need. It's crying out to them, demanding to make them mine. *How can one deny that?*

Maxwell takes me from Knox and kisses me. I can hear Beasty rumbling in his chest and my pleasure ramps up again. He must notice because he does it again and then dives in to take my lips in a brutal kiss. I'm gasping for air when he finally pulls away and flips me on my stomach. He leans over and swipes my hair to one side. "Usually I would take my time and drive you to the edge of insanity before I gave you what you want, but it seems Beasty wants you now. Hard and fast, sweetheart. So hang on and enjoy the ride." Before I can so much as nod my agreement and understanding, he is slamming home and rips a low and needy filled moan from my throat. Holy shit. He is reaching spots I didn't think were possible with this new position. I fist the black silk sheets in my hands and hang on like he said as he continues a brutal pace that has me seeing stars by the time our climaxes hit. When he finally relaxes, he runs his fingers down my spine, not caring that I have rough and torn patches of skin. He pulls himself out and Cas is there, rolling me over to face him.

My body is exhausted, and I can feel sweat dripping off my body and soaking the bed. He leans over and kisses me tenderly, but his delicate touch leaves me confused. He picks me up and walks to the bathroom and I pout because I thought I would be getting at least one more orgasm before I slept for like a week straight. He grins in response and I give him a death stare, knowing he heard my inner thoughts again. *I really need to learn how to shut that shit off.*

"Don't worry, baby girl. You're still getting one, but you also need to be cleaned and the others are going to change the sheet for you." I smile at that. I really didn't want to sleep on dirty sheets. "You did such a good job, baby girl. Taking all of us in one night." I feel him reach over and turn on the water and then step into the shower without putting me down. Which is fine because I'm pretty sure my legs are jelly. *Who knew sex with six guys is the equivalent to a full on gym work out. I didn't.*

He holds me tight to his chest for a long moment until he shifts us and I'm straddling him with his hands on my ass to hold me up. "I'm sorry, baby girl." I frown at him, not understanding what he is apologizing for. "I wasn't there to protect you. I have made so many mistakes when it comes to you. I don't deserve you." Magic stirs in my chest, peeking at him. She flashes me an image of me against the wall and Cas fucking me in the shower as I scream out his name and I couldn't agree more with her right now. I reach up and rest my forehead against his with my hands on his cheeks.

"There was nothing you could have done. I saved myself and with that, I made myself a stronger person. Without my past I would have never met you guys. Don't blame yourself for something out of your control." I press my lips to his in a tender kiss. "Now, are you going to show me how sorry you are or do I need to ask one of the others to?" He growls as he looks between my eyes as I cock a brow in a "well, what are you waiting for" look. He turns us so my back is against the shower wall and slams into me. His eyes didn't waver from me and I felt him ease into my embrace as I drew him closer. We move together, not fighting for dominance, but moving as one. Not even rushing as I feel the tell-tell signs of my climax building. "Cas." I moan and he leans into my neck and kisses me. He whispers something that I swear sounded like, "I love you." But that's not right. Before I can over think it, magic builds in my chest as my climax hits. Cas tumbles into the sweet bliss seconds after me and then I feel it.

It's like a locked door being kicked open. Pieces flying everywhere. Power floods my system and my blood heats to the point of fiery pain. I hear a groan and my eyes snap open, not realizing I even shut them. Black, red and gold strands of shadow and mist whip around the room. Caressing my skin and then Cas's. I hear the others groan and can only assume it is affecting them as well.

What is happening now? I swear to Hell if my magic tries to claim one more male, I will figure out a way to lock her up in a damn timeout. Yes, multiple orgasms and men to serve me is amazing, but I barely survived six in one night. There is just no way that I could do more. Cas shuffles us to the door, still in his arms and dripping wet and yup. All my men are wrapped in my insanely handsy magic. It glides across every inch of their skin in a loving touch, but this feels different from all the other times. This feels right. Like this is meant to be.

After a few moments of us staring at each other and the odd tingles my magic gave me as it caressed and swept over every inch of my skin, the air in the room changes. Like a vacuum tunnel, my magic swirls around my men and the room and then slams back into my chest, taking my breath away.

I faintly hear a few "oh shits," "fucks," and a "what the hell just happened?" but before I can even figure anything out a wave of dizziness hits and the abyss opens its arms again but this time it's a sweet warm embrace as my eyes close and the blackness consumes my mind.

EIGHTEEN

AZZIE

I could die a happy woman. Well, if a happy woman is sore in all the right places and her insides feel all warm and tingling. In a non-creepy way, of course. It's like a second pulse just under my skin. It's strange but not unpleasant. It seems to bring a feeling of ease, like this was always meant to happen. My magic. This warmth. These men being mine.

At the thought of my men and the night I just had, I jerk upright. Body sore, but in the most delicious way. I swipe my hand across the sheets next to me and realize that they are cold. I frown. *Why wouldn't they stay with me?* I look around, thinking maybe they are in the bathroom or around the room, but the room is quiet and not a sound can be heard. A deep pain stabs through my chest like a hot iron poker against my skin. *Why would they just leave me after everything we did together last night? Were they just lies?* I thought... I thought... my thoughts are cut off as the bedroom door slams open and in rushes six men with a wide range of emotions on their faces. Panic, fear, worry and then relief, awe, and love replaces the first set of emotions when they see that I'm okay.

"Baby girl." Cas breathes in an almost whisper. He steps forward and scoops me in his arms. "We would never leave you. We wore you out and wanted you to sleep while we made you breakfast and spoke with your dad and Birdy." He kisses my forehead and lingers for a second, inhaling my scent as if just breathing me in relaxes him. I realize it's still weird how gentle this man is with me after how he treated me when I first came to town, but deep in my bones, I know he belongs to me and I've never been great at sharing.

My brows furrow for a second. *How did they know I was having a minor freak out?* My magic peeks up again, sending a swirl of black, red and gold across my eyes as I see magic whips connected to my guy's chest and I feel this overwhelming possessive feeling. *Mine.*

"Yes, Kitten. We are yours." Max says next to my ear as Beasty purrs and sends pleasant shivers down my back. I blink and the magic fades from my sight.

"What were those?" I ask, not really to anyone in particular. I look around the room at all the confused faces. "The magical whip things connected to your chests leading back to mine." I point to each of their chests and then back to mine as if they couldn't comprehend my words. Cas lifts a brow in questions. "They were red, black and gold shadowy whips. Like that day, my hussy magic claimed you guys." Someone snorts, and I think I hear someone mumble about what hussy magic is. "Honestly, it was like a leash that tied you to me. Awe. Do I have to take you guys for walks and feed you? Or maybe scratch behind your ears? Grim and Reaper really like that." I smirk, knowing that would piss one or more guys off, but to my surprise Kam and Cain take a step forward as if not realizing and then I see the orange flames in their eyes. "Yup, I think they liked that idea." I say with a laugh. My laugh must have broken their hound's control because they both shake their head and then blush.

"Holy shit. Did my little rebel just make you guys blush? Ha."
Remi says in between laughter. I smile big then. My unease from
earlier washing away. I have to get used to this whole someone else
feeling my emotions thing and me feeling theirs because I keep getting
waves of lust and I don't know how long I can hold out until I jump
one of them again. It's like they unlocked a part of me I didn't know
existed. But Princess Azzie is beyond sore and need a solid few days
of rest.

Suddenly laughter erupts around me and my face turns bright red
and I throw myself into the bed and cover my face. "Stay out of my
head!" I yell, but I'm laughing as well.

After embarrassing myself with naming my lady parts, Princess
Azzie, which I find completely reasonable, by the way. *If guys can
nickname their dicks, why can't I nickname my lady parts? It's only
fair.* We headed out into the kitchen where a feast fit for a queen
and her kings was set up on the dining room table. I look around,
confused. "What are you looking for, my queen?" Knox slides up
behind me, kissing the top of my head.

"Where are Birdy and my dad?" I ask, still looking around. Birdy
has to be here if this much food was made.

"What did you need, Kitten? Grandma and Michael left for the
night to give us privacy and will stop by later." I frown after Max's
statement. He smirks. "Oh, I see. You didn't think she didn't teach

us how to cook over the years? She told us that our queen would enjoy food and that we should learn to cook to impress her. Well, you." His cheeks show a small blush, and my heart skips a beat. *Did they really learn to cook just for me?* "Plus, Remi is a bottomless pit and the hellhound twins can eat your weight in food in one seating, so it would save in take out cost." *Well, that was romantic for half a minute.*

"Hey, I'm not a bottomless pit. I'm a growing boy." Remi exclaims and then flexes his muscles my way. I let a small chuckle. These guys were not what I expected when I first met them and but they are growing on me, I suppose.

I take my seat, which is apparently at the head of the table, while the guys take theirs. My mouth waters at the smell of eggs, bacon, sausage, french toast, waffles, hash browns, fresh fruit, and are those crepes? I fill my plate with a bit of everything when I realize no one else has moved. I look up and raise my brow. "What? Never seen a girl eat before. After last night, I need my energy for the future." I say and continue to build a mountain of food on my plate. I pop a piece of crispy bacon into my mouth and moan as the greasy goodness slides down my throat. All at once, the room goes silent and I look around again. "Oops." I smile wide and continue on.

After I settle my plate down in front of me, I make a game plan on how to tackle the yumminess that's piled high. "You know what would be amazing right now?" Before I can answer my own question, Remi is setting a large cup of God's gift to mortals next to me. He kisses my head and whispers, "Just the way you like it." I inhale the sweet and rich scent of coffee and have to hold back another moan. *Just perfect.*

Half way through breakfast, Birdy and Michael show up with approving smiles adorning their faces. Birdy winks at me and I smile big. I will have to hug that woman later and thank her for teaching the guys how to cook because I was stunned at how yummy all of it came out. They each grab a plate and eat while we all talk about nonsense and laughter rings out at each other's comments or stories being told. It's nice to see all the guys relaxed and at ease, but I know it won't last long and I'm proven right when Birdy pulls me to the side once we are all done. She tells the guys to clean up and they all hesitate before she spears them with a fierce glare and then they all snap to do what she says. *Maybe she can teach me her ways in the art of a glare.*

"How are you feeling, sweetheart?" She asks in that grandmotherly way that I've never experienced. I shrug. How do you even explain what I've been through lately? It's like I can't catch my bearings or even take a break. It's one thing after another and each thing I learn keeps getting worse.

Oh Azzie, you're supernatural, not human. The man that raised you is not your dad. He kidnapped you as a baby. Three years ago, you met your actual dad who had been looking for you since the day you were taken. Also, you're a queen of Hell and have five mates. Oh, and your sister wants to kill you. Did I say five mates? I'm sorry I meant six mates, not five. Did I say queen of Hell? I meant you're actually the queen of the Chaos realm that encompasses all supernatural ever created. Everything is fine. My world is totally not going up in flames. Haha, flames because Hell is supposed to have flames, but it's actually a paradise.

But of course I don't say any of that. "I'm fine. Just a lot, I guess." I shrug but come on, no woman has ever said "I'm fine" and really meant it.

She hums and gives me a soft smile. "Azzie, my dear, I have seen something and the boys must not know how it will play out. I can

also only be vague with you, but it may prepare you a bit as well."
I groan. *Damn it.* I already know this is going to suck. I wonder if
I hide my head in the sand like an ostrich. Will all my problems go
away? Probably not.

I take a deep breath, knowing I will have to figure out how to keep
the guys out of my mind as well. "Okay, but I need Mich-"

"Yes, dear, he will teach you a few things tonight that you will need
to know." She smiles and taps the corner of her eye. I slit my eyes at
her. *I wonder if anything gets past this woman.*

I nod. "Okay then." She takes my elbow in a gentle hold and leads
me to where my dad waits in a makeshift home gym the guys have.
The smell of sweat, worn down leather workout bags and cleaning
products fills my nose. *Home.* Living in a gym for three years with
Michael was the best years of my life. He taught me how to fight,
how to take a hit and give one twice as strong back. He also engrained
that I shouldn't bow to anyone. It makes tons of sense now, but back
then I thought they were just weird pep talks because he didn't know
what to do with a teenage girl instead of the big, bulking men who
worked out normally at his gym.

I smile big up at my dad, "I didn't know you were going to let me
kick your butt today, old man." He smirks and I start to rethink my
words as all the long nights of running drills and laps rush through
my mind. "Actually, you know what," cough, cough. "I think I might
be coming down with something." Cough, cough. I take a small step
back and he makes his move. He swipes his foot out, lightning fast, to
try and take out my ankles. I tried to jump and give him a roundhouse
kick to his right side, but he caught my leg before I could and, with a
heave of his arms, I went flying and ended up sprawled on the floor.
The sudden force steals my breath away, yet I can't help but laugh.
"I almost had you." He smiles widely.

"You weren't even close, but that's not the training we are doing today." I frown. "It will be training of your mind, little star. How to hide your power signature, among other things." I groan.

"I'd rather get beat up but you." He helps me up and hugs me tight. "Lets get this over with."

Nineteen

G rim purrs as Azzie reaches over and scratches behind his ear before kissing the top of his head. "Move over, big guy. I need to pee." She rushes to the bathroom and I'm right behind her. I move my snout to push open the door to make sure she is safe, but I freeze when I hear her next word. "Grim, if you step one paw into this bathroom while I'm taking a piss, I swear you will not get a single pet or tummy rub for an entire week. I'm perfectly safe here. Now step away from the door. You're making this awkward." I step back and sit on my haunches and laugh at our predicament. *Oh, how the mighty hellhound has fallen.*

Damn overprotective mutt. Ever since she fully mated with us and we felt her increase our powers, he has become a lovesick puppy. Wherever Azzie is, we need to be right there with her. Needless to say, the last few days at school have been rough and not just for me. Why did Birdy and Michael think it was a good idea that we all go back to school and continue to keep up this pretense? We aren't like the others here and Knox already said that Frank was on Azzie's trail. We should be miles away from here to protect her, but Birdy just says it will all work out.

School has been difficult, to say the least. We all want to be near her all the time and Azzie is now threatening us in new creative ways. Like withholding belly rubs and head scratches to Grim and Reaper. She even threatened Remi with no take out food for a year and told Cas she would rearrange his office and files if he didn't give her breathing room at lunch on Monday. The look of horror on his face was priceless, but being on the receiving end of these threats is terrifying. She is brutal with them and none of us are willing to test out if she will follow through or not.

When she is done and steps out, she gives us a look that screams, you can't be serious right now, but we give her our best wolfish grin and lick her thigh when she steps closer. "Ewww, gross. No drool." She yelps, but continues to scratch behind my ears anyway. "How about we go start breakfast?" Grim whines and gives her puppy eyes. He can't be serious. I push him back so I can take over and shift back into my human body. She already has a pair of shorts in her hands when I straighten myself.

"Hey angel." I lean in and grab her around the waist and pull her against me. "Miss me?" She giggles, and it's music to my ears.

"Breakfast. I worked up an appetite last night." The little brat winks at me and sashays her cute little ass away from me, humming a tone I hadn't heard before.

"Tease." I say under my breath. It shouldn't be allowed for her to walk around in one of our t-shirts and panties that barely cover the juicy round globes of hers. I readjust myself and pull on my shorts. The others are still asleep, but I give them thirty minutes before they either realize she is gone, hear her in the kitchen singing or smell the food.

I turn around and, like the good boy I am, I follow Azzie into the kitchen to watch as she swings her hips and sings her song while making coffee and breakfast. It's a hardship, I know, but one I would serve repeatedly.

There is a chill in the air that feels wrong today. We all know something is wrong and tried to talk Azzie out of going to school today, but she refused and threatened to take away sex if we tried to keep her from school and her friends. She then continued to give us each a kiss and then headed to Cas's SUV. We should have known something was up because she always rides her bike with Remi while we follow behind them. Looking back, we should have known.

Morning classes went by fine and with ease. There was a flyer and an announcement over the intercom that there was some type of assembly during sixth period that was mandatory, but I didn't think twice about it. I overheard a bunch of students talking about it and how the mayor was making some type of announcement about the town. I heard that there's going to be a wolf-related holiday soon. Not being a werewolf it didn't affect me, but all the students had to be present.

During lunch, I felt like I had eyes watching me. When I mind linked my brothers, they explained having the same feeling but none of us could identify where the feelings were coming from especially since we have had eyes on us since Monday when Knox joined the Kings and one or more of us were always attached to Azzie. Plus, we didn't make any effort to cover up our mate marks. We wore them with pride and made it a point to show them every chance we got. We got a ton of shocked faces and some furious ones from females when they realized we were all claimed by one woman. *To say the females of this school were not happy was an understatement.* We all had to continue to hide our power signature, especially my angel. She has been practicing with Michael since she came into full power and she has it down quite good. You would think she was still human if you didn't know any better.

Michael has been working with her on other things as well, but by the time she finishes working with him, she is exhausted and we have to help her into bed.

Today, she is sitting between Mac and Caleb while Ivy leans over. I know they can all mind link as well and for the most part they do, but the looks they keep giving her and each other has Grim even more on a razor thin edge. Something is not right; I can feel it and I think Azzie knows it.

During art class, I try to bring up why I feel like she is hiding something, but then she changes the topic by mentioning the things she wants to try in bed and I'm ashamed to admit that a whole other brain takes over. She smirks, knowing she was successful in her subject changing, but the unease that something is seriously wrong keeps crossing my mind.

"Hey, I'm fine. I promise. Like Birdy says, it will all work out in the end." She says as the end of the hour bell rings and we have to spilt for fifth period. "I will see you in an hour. Stop worrying." She winks at me and then smiles, but her smile seems forced. She is trying to make us feel at ease, however, what information is she privy to that we are not? She pivots, intertwining her arms with Mac, who had been waiting outside the door for her, and I focus on Cas with imploring eyes. He is our leader. He needs to figure out a game plan so we can prevent whatever is going to happen.

"I know." He says, staring after Azzie with a forlorn look. He hates being away from her as much as I do.

"She knows something, but won't tell us. I can't even get a read on her thoughts lately. It's like I'm hitting a brick wall." I almost let loose a whine from Grim but fight to swallow it back down. "Does she not think we can protect her?"

"I don't know, Kam, but I have a bad feeling about this assembly. We all need to be on alert. If anything is going to go down today, it's going to be during that." He nods to the door and I follow him out. He's right, but I have a feeling that we aren't going to like the outcome of this announcement.

TWENTY

AZZIE

I am such a shitty girlfriend, mate, or am I a wife now? Shit, did I get magically married somehow? I push that thought aside for now. I have more pressing matters at the moment.

Walking into the gym for the assembly feels like walking myself to the gallows. I mean, I know I'm not going to die, but the feelings the guys have been getting all day are real. We are being watched and I know exactly who is doing the watching. He is here.

All week, Michael and I have been training to the point of me being physically and mentally exhausted. We have gone over the plan for what feels like a million times, so many it is engrained into me now. Birdy's vision helped in many ways. I knew what to prepare for and we were able to train my mind for what was to come.

As we climb the bleachers, I see the guys scanning the area for threats. I know they won't find what they are looking for since the first threat is actually sitting at the bottom of the bleachers filing her nails as if she has no care in the world. Stupid, stupid Bella. She thinks she has the upper hand today, but even without Birdy and her all-seeing eyes, Bella wouldn't stand a chance against me. Not when what is mine is being threatened. Oh no, she is about to cross a line she is going to wish she had never drawn.

As I take my seat, my guys surround me as if guarding the crown jewels or the queen of England. Which is somewhat true since I'm sort of kind of supposed to be the queen of the Chaos realm. I nod to Caleb and Ivy as they flank Cas and Knox, who sit behind me. Kam and Cain are on either side of me, and Max and Remi are in front of me with Mac next to her brother, just in case.

Hiding and planning behind the guy's backs has been tough the last few days, but I only have one chance to get this right and I will not risk them in the process.

"Are you sure about this, Azzie?" Mac links me and I glance at her. She looks worried and I smile at her to try to set her at ease.

"Yes. I need you to be able to hold your brother off long enough for this to happen. You have to trust me." I plead. There is only one way this can work. *It has to work.*

"We trust you, Azzie. We just don't want to die when they realize what our part is in all this." Caleb gives a nervous chuckle into the link and I look over and smile at him as well and Cas growls low. I roll my eyes at his possessive growl. He knows Caleb bats for the home team, but my men still get all growly around him.

"Really Cas, you're jealous of Caleb, who would rather get into your pants than mine?" A pang of jealousy hit my chest, but I pushed it away because it was ridiculous to even consider. I know my friend would never make a move on my men, but the thought still makes me grimace. Cas looks like he might be sick. I giggle at that and his lips tip up into an almost smile. But he keeps his straight face in place..

The tap of a microphone and the principal welcoming everyone interrupts the moment. I look around one more time and met eyes with none other than the bitch queen herself. She smirks at me, then gives my men a once over. It takes everything in me not to jump up, charge over to her and punch her in the nose, so instead I bite my cheek and glare back. Once her eyes stop undressing my mates, she winks at me and I can't help myself. I smile wide, which makes her smirk fall for a second.

Yes, Bella, you should be afraid. You're about to make the worst mistake of your life.

I mind link my friends. "It's game time. Let's show this bitch how to bow."

The principal drones on about a few random things, from an upcoming school dance to tomorrow night's football game and how we are going to take the win all the way to state. *Whatever that means.* I've never been involved with school activities and didn't plan to start now. I wonder how my life would have been different if someone hadn't kidnapped me as a baby and then treated worse than gum on the bottom of someone's shoe.

After a few more minutes of ramblings, the principal finally announces a special guest has joined up today and would like to say a few words before the cheerleaders put on a show for their school sprint. *Thank Hellfire, I won't be here for that.*

"Lets all give a big welcome to Mayor Blackwood." Everyone claps as a man who looks to be about in his forties walks to the podium. He has dark brown hair, peppered with gray. Blue eyes and a clean-shaven face. He is dressed in a three-piece dark gray suit with a light blue tie that matches the blue of his eyes. He is handsome for someone his age and at first I can't fathom how Bella is related to this man. Cain chuckles next to me and leans in to whisper. "Bella takes after her mother." I hum in understanding. Watching as he settles in and waits for the crowd to quiet down.

"Thank you, thank you. As you may all know, I'm Mayor Blackwood and each year around this time, I visit you guys to let you all know about the upcoming Ash Valley Founders' Day celebration. It will be a grand festival to celebrate over a hundred years of being the beautiful town of Ash Valley. This year there will be a carnival with fun games and prizes to win. There will be tons of food booths and some great presentations on our town's history. So I encourage you all to join us for a fun filled day." He says with bright eyes and a wide smile. He seems like a decent man and I know the guys told him who I am as well, at least who they thought I was at the time. None of us knew it was a lot bigger than just the queen of Hell, a small portion of the Chaos Realm. *No, I had to go and be the rightful queen of Chaos.* Fitting, since the guys have always called themselves the Chaos Kings. *I should really ask them why they chose that name.*

From the corner of my eye, I see Bella raise her perfectly manicured hand up high. Her dad, Mayor Blackwood, smiles soften at her. His love for his daughter is obvious, but I don't think he realizes what she is about to get herself into. "Yes, Bella. Do you have a question?" He nods for her to ask.

"Daddy, is it true that according to supernatural laws and customs that if someone feels they have been wronged or that someone has taken something that doesn't belong to them they can challenge that person in front of their peers for the right to own what is and should be rightfully there's?" She says in a sugary sweet, innocent voice and

I smile. Mayor Blackwood snaps his head to me and my men, who are now all growling.

"Bella, now is not the time nor place to discuss this." He hisses at her, giving her a stern look to drop the subject.

She bats her lashes and continues to speak in that sugar sweet tone that makes me feel nausea when I hear it. "But daddy. I only want to ensure that my fellow students and peers know the laws and customs of our kind. Soon we will all be adults and need to learn these things. Is it true you can challenge someone if you feel they have wronged you?" She asks again, and I can see the sweat building on the mayor's forehead. He is worried for his daughter and in all honesty, he should be, but her reign of terror needs to end and this must play out so all the other little chess pieces can fall into place.

Mayor Blackwood looks over at me again. Pleading with his eyes to show his daughter mercy. I nod my head in understanding. He must see something in my face because he takes a deep breath and looks back at the crowd, knowing that once he answers Bella's question, she will no doubt make a claim and a fool of herself.

He clears his throat and adjusts his tie, only delaying the inevitable. "To answer your question, Bella, yes. You may request a challenge if you feel another has wronged you with the audience of your peers to bear witness. Our people have long since used this custom. It is also recommended to seek council before you make such claims against another as most challenges are to the death." He almost ends in a growl, trying to once again warn his daughter to stand down, but in her twisted mind, she truly believes my kings should belong to her.

Monday when Knox joined us for the first day back, every girl's eyes watched him. I mean, who couldn't keep their eyes off any of my men? With my little power up flowing through them, they almost seem to glow and command that all eyes stay on them. Of course, that got me even more death glares because these damn guys can't keep their hands off me. I'm not complaining, but it was hilarious when Bella approached Knox in the hall right before lunch, pressing her chest out to show her cleavage and batting her lashes so hard, I thought she was going to create a brisk wind stream with them. I just stood there watching, knowing Knox sensed me a mere few feet away. She leaned in to whisper something to him, and I had no doubt she was trying to seduce him somehow. Once she was done spewing her poison, he simply pulled up the sleeve of his long shirt bearing his mate mark, then smiled widely and turned towards me. If looks could kill, I would have been murdered a hundred times over. He walked over to me and kissed me so deeply that I totally forgot Bella was next to us fuming. After a minute, I just winked at her and watched as she spun on her to tall heels and stormed off.

Zoning back into the gym and my surrounding I see Bella stand from the bottom of the bleachers. "Bella, take a seat. We will talk about this later." Her dad grinds out to her, still trying to maintain his Mayor Blackwood composer, but Bella ignores him and turns towards the crowd.

My guy's all tense, realizing finally what is about to happen. Cain and Kam grip my hands tighter and I feel the other press in close to either comfort me or maybe themself.

Bella stands there while the gym goes dead silent, waiting with bated breath. She straightens her spine and then looks at all my men. I managed to stay silent, barely restraining my contemptuous feelings, until her eyes met mine with a vicious look. "I, Bella Maria Blackwood, would like to challenge Azzie Mornings in front of an audience of our peers, for the right to claim her supposed men that she forced into mating her with some type of black magic." I am powerless to resist the eye roll I give her at her claims. She continues on like the men in question aren't raging by my side at the audacity of the crazy bitch. "They were in the process of courting me, but once Azzie came to town, they all became different. She bewitched them and then forced them into a mate bond with her."

I let out a laugh. My laughter is so strong it causes a tear to roll down my face and I wipe it away. I'm sure I look crazy and probably sound like a crazy witch crackling, but I really just can't help myself. I knew Bella was dense, but come on. When I finally calm down and can breathe, I look around at my men and shrug. "What? That was funny." I finally turn to the rest of the crowd and a very red-faced Bella. "Those are some serious accusations you're throwing out. I believe you should take your father's advice and seek council before you decide to challenge me." I say in a calm tone, a 180-degree change of the laughter fit I just went through a moment ago, but I know how this will play out already.

Bella looks over at her dad who is glaring at her and if I'm not mistaken mind linking her, but oh no, Bella Blackwood thinks she is the queen B of this school and deserves to get what she wants. "I have spoken with a council; now do you accept my challenge or not?" She grinds out. If I didn't know she was a wolf shifter, I would have guessed a snake shifter with how much venom she is spitting my way.

Before any of my guys can object, I swiftly stand, lift my head higher and let my lip form a wicked smile. "I accept your challenge." My men growl, but I silence them with a hand held up. "Now let's make this bitch bow to a real queen."

TWENTY-ONE

REMI

I don't know whether I should be pissed or proud of Azzie for going through with this stupid little challenge? I mean, I know there is no way in Hell's crown she can lose, not with her power being unbound now but still. No one ever wants to see their mate being challenged over someone who is really just a petty ass bitch.

Azzie smiles back at Bella with a wicked grin. "I accept your challenge." She then looks over towards us and smirks. "Now let's make this bitch bow to a real queen." I give her a lopsided grin in return. *Damn, she is hot when she gets this way.* She leans down and grabs Max by the back of the head, then presses her lips to his in a hard and rough kiss. *Fuck, that's hot.* When she is done, she looks over at me and proceeds to kiss me with just as much passion, but it's over far too soon.

One by one, she kisses each of us with passion and something else I can't quite put my finger on, but it's a powerful emotion. I know lately she has been training a lot with Michael and she has been learning how to block her thoughts from us. I don't like it, but I get the need for privacy when you have six men who are constantly begging for attention. We are like a gang of puppy dogs, just wanting to please our owner. Make no mistake Azzie owns us. Heart, body, and soul.

When she gets to Cas, she pauses and with that wicked smile still plastered on her plush lips; she looks over at a now red faced and fuming Bella. If I didn't know better, I would have said there was smoke coming out of her ears like you see in cartoons. Azzie leans in and kisses Cas like this was the last kiss she was ever going to give him. Bella growls out but we all ignore her, but from the corner of my eye I see Bella's dad pull her aside and start speaking to her with rapid hand movements. We know he can't tell her why she just made the biggest mistake of her life because of the binding agreement we made with him.

"All right, boys. Be good and sit still while I show this dog how to heel." Azzie winks at us as she saunters down the steps of the bleachers. I can't help that my eyes zero in on her plump, round ass. *God damn, that's a nice ass.* I have to shift in my seat and readjust myself.

Azzie walks to the middle of the gym and stands with her head held high, spine as straight as a steel rod and smirks at us like she has no worries in the world. Bella walks over to the center of the gym almost as confident as my little rebel, but I can see the glint of doubt in her eyes as she eyes my woman with disdain. Mayor Blackwood walks between the girls and gives Azzie a pleading look. Maybe begging her to give his stupid daughter some type of mercy.

Blackwood faces the audience, looking nervous and unsure of this entire situation, but straightens and clears his throat. "A challenge has been issued, and the challenge has been accepted." He gestures to first Bella and then Azzie. He pauses, looking a bit uncertain, then he lifts his eyes to the crowd and announces, "The prize of this challenge will be. . ." Pausing again, he takes a deep breath and continues.

"The prize of this challenge will be the right to claim Caspian, Remi, Cain, Kamdon, and Maxwell as mates. The terms of..." Before he can continue on, Bella interrupts with her annoying high pitch whine of a voice.

"Knox as well, daddy. He is a part of the kings and should be mine as well." She smiles up at us like she is hot shit and actually has a chance to win this. I sneer down at her, but she must not see it or just doesn't care.

"Do we not have a say in who we choose to mate?" Cas growls out, and the gym seems to freeze and all eyes turn to us but come on, they had to know we wouldn't go along with this. *Azzie is our fated mate. This isn't a choice, fate herself wrote it in the stars.*

"Well, I suppose you do, but the challenge must play out before you may have that say. Because of the setting and the short notice of this challenge, the terms are whoever admits defeat first or who-ever is too injured to continue on will be considered the loser. The winner will be allowed to choose these men as their mates. It is my understanding that mate marks have been issued. If miss Mornings is defeated, these marks will be removed and Bella may claim these men as hers." He looks over again at Azzie and she gives him a quick nod and I see his shoulders sag in what seems like relief. *What is that about?*

"The rules are simple. There will be no killing of any sort. You may use magic or your shifting ability, but no killing blows. Injuries can and will occur, but there will be no interference by anyone unless you admit defeat. Once defeat is admitted by a contender, the other must back away immediately. Do you both understand?" He looks over at Azzie first, who nods again. *I know this is an easy win, but why isn't she fighting this more?*

I know she can wipe the floor with this bitch, but Azzie just seems resigned to something. Like she knows something we don't. She has been off all week, but we have been trying to give her space since we have bombarded her with one thing after another, but something seems off today.

Blackwood looks over at Bella, and her lips turn up into a bright smile as she turns and blows a kiss in our direction. *Disgusting.* She truly thinks she has this in the bag. Like she is going to walk away from this and we are just going to fall to her feet and worship her like we worship our queen. It's laughable, really, as there is only one woman any of us would bow to and she is staring at us with a smug smile.

"Ladies, please take your places on either side of the line." They both turn and face each other and Bella sneers over at Azzie, who returns her looks with a sweet smile of her own. She then proceeds to raise her hand and bring her middle finger up to her nose to scratch it. Basically flipping Bella off. *That's my girl.*

Bella sneers and begins to speak to Azzie, but she is too far and the room is too loud with the excitement of a fight for any of us to hear her. Blackwood turns back towards the crowd and raises his hands to get everyone's attention once more. I didn't even realize that everyone else has their phones out and were ready to film the drama about to unfold. "The challenge will begin when I count down from three." He looks at the girls again, who seem to still be in a stare off. "Three." He looks back to the bleachers. "Two." Azzie looks back towards all of us and winks. "One." My body stiffens, not ready to see this throw down when Bella swipes a clawed hand across Azzie stomach. I except pain to sear my stomach but nothing. I look over at the others, confused, but they are looking around at each other, just as perplexed as me.

What is going on? I look back at the challenge as I see Bella try to strike Azzie again, but she deflects and wipes the blood from her stomach with a grimace. Nope. This doesn't work for me. Azzie looks over at us suddenly and mouths the word "now". *Now what?*

A heavy pressure settles over me, and my muscles tense up, making me unable to move. *What the hell?* I'm only able to move my head to check on the others, but see that they are equally frozen in place. From the corner of my eye, I can see Caleb whispering his magic. *That fucker.* Mac turns around and gives us a sad look. "It has to be this way. You have to trust her. I'm sorry." *What the fuck does she mean it has to be this way? That we have to trust her?* I turn to face my queen as she leans over Bella, who is now trembling on the floor. I forget all about my lack of movement for the moment and focus on my woman.

That's my rebel.

Twenty-Two

AZZIE

"Ladies, please take your places on either side of the line." I turn and walk over to the center of the court and face Bella with a smile. She sneers over at me. "I am going to destroy you and when I'm done, those guys will belong to me." I roll my eyes at her statement.

"Bella. I knew you were dense, but let's get one thing straight. You will bow to me when this is all said and done." My smile doesn't drop because I know exactly how this will end and I'm really not looking forward to it, but to save my guys, I'll endure it. Hopefully, they will get their shit together after.

"The challenge will begin when I count down from three." Mayor Blackwood says, and looks over at us as we face down. "Three!" He looks back to the bleachers where my guys all have a wide range of emotions. Worry. Annoyance. Anger. Fear. "Two!" I give each of my men a long look, then finish with a wink. I got this; I try to say with my eyes, but I don't know if it comes through. "One!"

I turn back towards Bella when my body tenses at her next words. "Frank says hi." She swipes her clawed hand out and I'm slow to move out of the way. Blood rushes down my stomach, but I keep my magic tight so the guys can't feel my pain. *Damn it.* I look over at them, knowing they are already on edge; I make eye contact with Caleb. "Now" I mouth.

Before this assembly started, I spoke with Caleb, Ivy, and Mac. I explained a few things and laid out my plan. At first I knew they were against the idea, but this is how it has to play out. Caleb nods and begins his spell for containing my men. They can't follow me through the portal right away. This only works if they come at the right time. I see them tense and then frown. *I hope they forgive me.*

I turn back to this damn annoying bitch who is now growling like a damn overgrown dog. *Oh wait, she is one.* I smirk at my thoughts as she tries to swipe at me once again. This time at my face. I give her a vicious grin. "Time to play then." I say and swing my right arm back at her and hit her right in the stomach. She grunts and bends over, grunting at the pain. She looks up and glares at me.

She continues to swipe at me left and right, missing each and every time and getting more and more pissed at the fact she can't land a hit, while I continue to dance around her like this is just a game. I land a few blows here and there, but I'm biding my time. "How does it feel to issue a challenge that you had no chance of winning?" I goad. "For men who want nothing to do with you."

"They are mine, you bitch. I can't wait for you to be put in your place by Frank. The things he said he wants to do to you." She snarls back. I straighten my spine at that. Frank can't hurt me anymore. I know that, but the memory of when I was helpless and alone floods my mind, giving Bella the chance to charge me. She shifts mid-jump, aiming her jaws at my throat, and that snaps me out of my dark thoughts. I spin out of the way at the last second, shaking my head to clear the rest of the terrible memories from my mind. *Now is not the time to take a walk down bad memory lane.*

I've been waiting for this, for her to shift, and now it's time to make a statement. I face the wolf version of Bella head on. If I didn't think Bella was a horrible and self-centered overgrown child who thinks all the toys in the sandbox should be hers, I would think her wolf was kind of cute. She is a tan and chocolate brown wolf that has white at the bottom of her paws and it looks like she is wearing little wolf socks. I would totally try to pet her and call her a good girl if she wasn't snarling and showing off her pretty white fangs towards me. She takes a step towards me, watching me and waiting for the right time to attack. I know she isn't aiming to just harm me, no that throat attack was meant to kill. I raise my hands calmly. "Bella, I know we got off on the wrong foot and all, but I really don't want to make you sit, stay, and roll over in front of all your friends. So, I'm giving you this chance to walk away with your wolf intact and the chance to still have some sort of dignity." If I'm being honest, I hope she tries to attack. My magic coils in my chest, preparing for what we both know is going to happen, but we thought we would give her the chance to change her fate. She chooses not to and lunges for me again. Magic wipes out of me and towards Bella before she even has a chance to dodge. It wraps around her, making her freeze mid leap. Gasps sound around the gym. *Oh yeah, no one really knew I had magic. Time for a showstopper then.*

"Bella Blackwood, I have given you a chance to forgo my wrath, but you seem hellbent on feeling it. Now please sit." Her wolf sits back on its haunches and cocks its head at me. I grin because I can't help myself. I walk over and pet the little wolf behind the ear. She can't move, but her eyes glare up at me. I lean into her and whisper, "Bella, I warned you. You would bow to me one day not because I'm queen bee of the school, and not because I'm the queen of the Chaos Kings that you desire to be yours, but because I was born to be the

CHAOS QUEEN: THE LOST QUEEN DUET

Chaos Queen. Now, bow bitch." Her eyes widen as her body does as I say. Helpless to disobey. Her wolf gets to its belly and stretches its legs out and throws its butt in the air. It's kind of funny to watch a wolf bow, but the satisfaction feels great.

I release my hold on her, but her wolf must realize my magic mean business right now and stays low in respect. I face the audience, who look like they can't believe what they're seeing. Surveying the room, my posture proud, I'm ready to take claim of my men when the most obnoxious voice assaults my ear drums. "You fucking bitch. How dare you!"

"I really didn't want to do this, but you left me no choice." I wave my hand at her and she freezes mid-step. I tilt my head down, pointing to the ground, and she falls to her knees. I bring my palms together and then slowly move them away from one another. Bella lets loose a god's awful scream as I forced her wolf to split from her. After a minute or two, Bella is bent over panting and trying to suck in air and next to her lays a tan and chocolate brown wolf staring up at me in confusion. "Now little wolf, you may run free until Bella learns to behave herself." The wolf nods in understanding like I knew it would. Their souls are still linked, but she will not be able to shift until I decide to reconnect their bodies. My magic will keep the little wolf safe till then, but Bella needs to learn a hard life lesson. Done with her and preparing myself for what is about to happen, I turn to face the bleachers once again.

My men are staring at me in awe and pride and the other students in fear. *Whatever.* "The challenge is over." Mayor Blackwood looks at me, and then over at his daughter, worry clear in his expression. "Mayor Blackwood, Bella is fine. She simply can't shift until she learns how to treat others with kindness and respect. Her wolf will be free to roam nearby and will be kept safe until further notice." His shoulder sag and nods in understanding.

Suddenly, the air in the gym shifts and sways. *It's time.* I look over at my men and give them a small smile. I nod to Mac. She knows what to do after this. A portal opens behind me and Frank appears with a smirk on his ugly face. James, Mayor Blackwood's beta, roars and charges towards me. "You bitch. I should kill you for what you did to her, but Frank and your sister will do it for me." He growls out and I prepare for the hit. I take one last look over at my men, my mates. "I'm sorry." I say before James collides with me and I'm pushed into the dark abyss once again.

TWENTY-THREE

CAIN

S hock, awe, and then pride runs through me as I see Bella panting on the ground and a wolf appear next to her. I was shocked, to say the least, when Bella and her wolf separated and the once put together soul now stood there in two. Just Bella and her wolf. "Now little wolf, you may run free until Bella learns to behave herself." Azzie tells the wolf and as if understanding, it turns and trots off out of the gym.

Azzie turns and faces all of us. "The challenge is over." Mayor Blackwood looks between the two in worry, but he is lucky that my mate is kind and didn't just end Bella when she tried to go for her neck. "Mayor Blackwood, Bella is fine. She simply can't shift until she learns how to treat others with kindness and respect. Her wolf will be free to roam and be kept safe until further notice." He nods in understanding and I know he wants to go to her, but he stays put.

I want to go to my mate as well, but Caleb continues to hold us down. Mac told us they had to ensure we stayed put, and that we needed to trust Azzie. I know I'm not the only one who wanted to interfere during this pointless challenge, but disabling our movements was unnecessary. Suddenly, the air in the gym becomes thick and over baring, like tar being dumped on me. *Something is wrong.* This isn't Azzie's magic, no, this is darker.

A roar rings out, and I snap my head to the sound. James Blackwood's beta is charging towards Azzie, who isn't moving. *Why isn't she moving?* I want to yell out to her, run to her, protect her, but Caleb continues to hold us hostage. "You bitch. I should kill you for what you did to her, but Frank and your sister will do it for me." A portal opens up behind Azzie and a man appears with a wicked smirk on his face. James' words finally register in my mind. No!

Azzie looks over at us and my heart breaks. She knew this was coming and didn't tell us. "I'm sorry." She says a second before James collides with her smaller body and she is pushed into the portal. Frank smirks once again, but this time it's aimed right at us, taunting us, then steps through behind her.

I stare at the portal as it closes, and Azzie is no longer standing there. The weight of Caleb's magic lifts as if it was never there and Reaper roars his fury to the room. My brother and Max do the same. I whirl around on him, ready to rip him to shreds, but Cas already has him by the throat. "Sh-She has a p-plan. Tr-trust her." He chokes out. Mac and Ivy get between Caleb and Cas, raising their hands as all six of us descend on them as one. *How dare they keep us from our mate?*

Mac speaks next. "Stop. You hurt us, you hurt her. We are just as connected to her as you are. Listen to us. She has a plan and we need to prepare for it. She didn't tell you because she knew you wouldn't let her go, but in order for all this to work, she had to go before us. Trust her." Reaper huffs in my chest. The sounds around us start to filter back in and then I remember I can take my anger out on someone else. The others must realize my thoughts because we turn as one and my eyes narrow in on James. He is cradling that stupid bitch who started this all.

I knew something was up with him. The day we met with Blackwood in his office, Beta James seemed off to my hound and I. We should have known Bella would try something to get the edge over Azzie. She thought getting with the beta would give her power. She didn't care about his age or that he was a married man. Oh no, Bella cares about power. I should have looked more into him; I could have prevented this. I could have figured out he was working with Frank, who has been after Azzie for a while now. But I was so focused on finding her at the time that I pushed him to the back of my mind. Now Azzie is gone. Again. Mac and the others know more information about Azzie and her top-secret plan, but I can't focus on that right now. James needs to hurt for what just happened, and I volunteer to serve up the pain.

I start towards the middle of the gym where he continues to hold Bella while she cries. Pulling the poor me card. She asked for this. Azzie gave her an out, but Bella truly thought she was superior to our queen. *How the mighty bitch has fallen.*

I reach the bottom of the bleachers on a mission to rip this piece of shit apart. My brother's right along with me, as Reaper shifts under my skin, begging to come out and play. We surround the two of them and Bella stiffens and looks up at us with her makeup running down her face, making her look like a raccoon or something. "You." I growl and Max grabs James by the back of his shirt, dragging him away from Bella as she finally looks at us in fear and not lust. I step over Bella and get into James' face, barely containing my growl, "When did you start working with Frank?" He looks at me and then scoffs. *Oh, this fucker thinks this is a game.* "Out." I growl to the room and turn and face the bleachers. No one moves.

Knox steps forward, rage vibrating from him. "He said out." He roars, the sound deafening, and shadows begin to leak from his hands and slide to the floor, edging to the stands. Everyone knows the Shadow kind are dangerous, but no one has ever dealt with them in this realm till recently. The crowd snaps out of their stunned state and starts hurrying towards the exits in fear of the shadows inching closer to them, waiting to suck them into a living nightmare until it drains them of life. Rumors, of course, but effective it seems. Maybe Knox fits in with us better than we thought.

I wait till everyone has made an exit before I turn back to the target for my rage. Bella at his feet, balling, and Mayor Blackwood inching closer. To save his daughter or defend his beta? Let's find out. I jerk my head in his direction and he flings his arms up in defense. "I just want to take Bella away before you rip him apart."

"Even your alpha finds you are a traitor. You became a traitor, all for what? A she-wolf who was using you for power because she couldn't have who she really wanted. You are a disgrace to the supernatural kind. You just sent the true queen to Hell's throne into the unknown without her guard, without her mates. You better hope she survives or the supernatural kind could soon perish, but you won't be here to witness it." I lean in towards him so he can see his death in my eyes. "When did you start working with Frank?" He looks over to his alpha as if he will help him, but Blackwood has already turned his back on him while he rushes to pick Bella's limp form up and moves away.

He surveys us with a calculating gaze, but the intensity and power that surrounds us must make him reconsider. "He approached me roughly a month ago. He requested that I keep an eye on her. That she was here to take down my pack. I believed him after she attacked

Bella and went after you all. Bella said she bewitched you all and that she was using dark magic." I scoff at that.

"Bella attacked Azzie then, like she did today. Azzie only ever defended herself. Bella is lucky Azzie was lenient with her. We wouldn't have been so merciful. Azzie had every chance and right to end Bella today, yet she let her off easy." Kam growls out through clenched teeth.

All of us are balancing on the edge of a sharp blade and without Azzie to ground us and rein us in, we are teetering. I'm afraid to see what will happen if we don't get her back this time.

I grab both sides of his head and twist sharply. Snap. Max lets go and James drops to the ground. That wasn't as satisfying as I wish it could be, but he deserved his end. I just wish I had time to prolong his suffering.

"Now what?" Remi asks, and for the first time, I have no idea. I look over to Cas and he looks just as lost as me.

"He had to of taken her to Hell. Frank is loyal to Margo, and she still thinks she can steal Azzie's powers. Her birthday is days away and knowing what I do of her, she will make it a grand affair. She will find a way to flaunt her newly gained powers." Knox says with a scoff.

"Your right that she is in Hell now and that Margo plans to make it a grand affair." Ivy says quietly as she, Mac, and Caleb approach us with caution. "She knows what she is doing. You all have to trust her for this all to work." She looks over at James and shivers, then eyes all of us. "We have lots to plan in the coming days." She nods to us or maybe to herself and turns, but stops and looks over her shoulder. "Well, are you coming?" I look over at the others and can see their determination to get our woman back. I turn and follow behind them.

Margo better be ready because I'm ready to burn Hell to the ground to get my woman back. Reaper rumbles inside my chest to agree.

Ready or not, here comes the Chaos Kings.

Twenty-Four

AZZIE

Ugh. This place again. I'm floating in the dark, bleak abyss again. I feel no pain but I also don't feel right. Something is missing, like I have a hole inside my chest. The emptiness feels wrong, its cold and makes me feel alone, but I know I'm not. My men will come for me. I know they will. This plan has to work or it will all be for nothing.

"Daughter, it's time to wake up." A sweet and soft voice calls out. Familiar, but not at the same time. "Open your eyes, darling. You have come home." *Home?* I've never felt like I've ever had a home.

With Frank, that was an endless time of moving around and what felt like torture for years. When I came across Michael, that was simply a stable roof over my head. Even when I moved to Ash Valley, I never felt like it could be like home, not till recently at least. My men feel like home. They have been my comfort and their arms have been my safe place, but I knew it wasn't going to last.

"My love, is she okay?" There was a deep voice coming from the other side of me. I attempt to move, but the darkness has me in its grip. I try to speak, try to move, anything but nothing happens.

Suddenly, a familiar warmth surrounds me, and the tips of my toes begin to tingle. The feeling inches up my body like it's melting away the icy cold feeling I had a minute ago. Ever so slowly, I'm able to flex my fingers and twitch my nose. "Time to open those pretty eyes, darling." The sweet voice that I'm pretty sure belongs to my mother says and I finally peek open my eyelids. It's still darkish and everything seems blurry, but as my eye's focus, I realize it's just the room that I'm in. *If you could even call it a room.*

I sit up, disoriented for a second, when my brain finally catches up with me. Bella. The assembly. The challenge that I won, of course. Me taking away Bella's wolf. Frank arriving with the portal to take me to Hell. James, charging towards me. The look of horror and anger on my king's faces. I worry they will freak out and ruin my plan, but Mac and them know what to tell the guy. I just hope that they trust what I need to do. *This can only play out one way, I'm afraid.*

I blink away the fog once I get a good look around. The room I'm in is actually a cell. *Perfect.* I'm laid out on a cot that is against a stone wall. To my left is a smaller wall which hides a toilet on the other side. At least I can pee in private, small mercies, I suppose. In front of me is the metal door to my new home. It looks solid, but I'll probably check it out once I get my bearings. To my right is another stone wall, much like the one on my left, but this wall has a window to the cell next to mine. Holding on to the bars in the window is a woman with a sad smile on her face and eyes a light pale gray color, almost white. Eyes that bore into mine like a million things need to be said. I can't believe the whispered word that slips pass her lips. "Daughter." I can't tell if she is asking me or stating what I'm almost positive is the truth. I'm frozen once again, but this time it's in outer shock.

"Mother?" I know I state my word as a question, but the shock of seeing the woman that I was told I killed somehow is disorientating.

I grew up imagining this woman. I dreamed of warm arms that were wrapped around me when I was sad. Coming home from school to someone who made sure I was fed and clean every night and made me chocolate chip cookies for when I was a good girl. I grew angry at this woman for leaving me with Frank and now I stare at her, knowing the truth. She sacrificed her life for me. Yeah, I grew up with a monster of a man, pretending to be my father, but every scar he left on my body strengthened me in the end. I step closer to her, needing to make sure she is real, but pause when I hear a door open from outside of my cell and down a way. The woman's eyes widen and nods back to the cot, a pleading look in her eyes. *Does she want me to lie down again?* I look back at her, unclear of her plea, until I hear a cruel laugh that I'm all too familiar with.

Frank.

I rush to the cot and pretend I never woke up. Just as I'm closing my eyes and slowing my breathing, I hear a key entering a lock. My magic peeks up from inside my chest, urging me to put this man in his place for once and for all, but I manage to contain the urge for now. I remind myself he will get his in due time, but we have to wait and follow the plan for all this to work. *It has to work.*

"So much for being some powerful supernatural. The portal still has her knocked out cold. Should we still bring her to her majesty?" An unfamiliar voice says. Someone suddenly kicked my cot, but I continued to show no reaction. "She doesn't seem like much and what is with all those marks on her body?" The man continues, and a laugh sounds out around the room.

"That would be my handy work." He says with pride. The nerve of this man, being proud that he was able to bully and scar a child who he was twice the size of. "I watched this little flower grow up, and I was there to make sure the little rose never got her thorns. Queen Margo says I can have her after she gets what she wants from her." He says gleefully. Frank leans down and brushes a finger down my cheek in what he must think is a sweet caress, but he doesn't know this flower has grown and her thorns are very real now. I hold back the full body shiver. Praying to hold down the vomit that wants to expel in the wake of his disgusting touch.

Someone bangs on the metal bars somewhere behind me, making Frank startle and pull away. I remain still, not wanting to give away my awaken state yet and my magic continues to push against my skin. It's only a matter of time until it breaks free and I'm worried about what it will do when that happens.

"Shut up, bitch. Queen Margo has things planned for all of you, but until then she is sending down gifts for you all. You will accept these gifts and join her for dinner tomorrow night. We have much to celebrate and she would enjoy some quality family time now that everyone is home." He laughs then, and it's a grating sound that I've heard many times before. He leans over once again and this time whispers in my ear. "My sweet little flower, I know you can hear me. Your sister has plans for you, but she promised me a little taste of your sweetness. I know you degraded yourself to those little boys. I can smell it, but don't worry, that just means I don't have to be so gentle with you." He licks my cheek and backs away, laughing, but my muscles are locked tight as I try not to race to the toilet and puke up my insides. I can hear yells and growls from other deep, low voices outside of my room, along with the banging of the metal bars from before, but I can't move.

With the loud clanking of the metal door shutting and the sound of the lock being set in place, I wait for an entire minute until I can't take the anticipation any longer. I quickly rise and dash to the side wall that conceals the tiny toilet. I managed to get there just before my stomach begins to heave. I can't remember the last time I ate, and hardly anything came up, so it must have been a while ago. My chest throbs with the beat of a war drum, calling me to action, while my stomach continues to heave. I refuse to fear Frank anymore, not with my magic buzzing under my skin, giving me the confidence of knowing I could take him easily. No, it's the fact that he touched me like he thought he had the right. My men come to mind then and how their touch makes me feel, and I imagine for a second that I'm surrounded by them. Their warmth, their scents and I wish they didn't have to see what must be done soon.

I drag myself up, not realizing that I sank to the ground at some point. I wipe my mouth clean and wish I had a toothbrush or even mouthwash. Apparently, dental hygiene is not at the top of the list for a prisoner. I straighten my clothes and take a deep breath, turning back to the eyes that mirror my own. My mother.

This time I step towards her with more confidence, knowing that this woman is the one who visited me in the abyss's darkness and guided me when I didn't know I needed it. When I reach the window, I see tears running down her cheek and I'm surprised for a second when she reaches out and wipes some away from my cheeks as well. *When did I start crying?* She smiles down at me but doesn't say a word. *What do you even say to a person you haven't seen in eighteen years?* I'm confused when another voice sounds from behind her.

"Margo took her voice the day of the attack. Mother would have been able to spell her or come up with a plan to escape with it." I'm shaking my head, because that can't be true. I've heard her voice before. She told me to wake up before Frank and that other guy showed up. I know I did.

I look over at the guy in confusion. I know my dad said that my mom had other mates, but this guy looks a few years older than me. *Surely supernaturals don't age that slowly.* "Who are you?" I ask because I didn't notice there was even anyone with her before. My mother looks over at the guy and nods her head. To my surprise, he walks through the wall and into my cell. I stumble back a bit stunned and apparently still not used to magic and the things people can do. He holds out his hand as if for me to take and at first I hesitate. Stranger danger and all that, but when I glance at my mother again, she nods in encouragement. I take the guy's hand and he pulls me through the wall as my magic stirs from the sudden odd feeling of going through a very solid wall. I gasp for the breath that was just sucked from me by the sudden movement, and a second later, I'm surrounded by a warm embrace and the smell of jasmine and vanilla. Mother.

"My names Jasper. I'm your older brother. Nice to finally meet you, Azzie. Sorry, it's not under better circumstances, but we have little time. Mother says you have a plan. Want to fill us in?" I stand there in shock at his statement. I can't help but nod my head up and down. Disbelief still coursing through me until I remember Michael saying I have an older brother, but can I trust him? I mean, my older sister wants to kill me for my power and crown. *Why wouldn't he want to, too?* I step back and away from him and my mother and the move must make sense to him, along with the suspicion that shows on my face, because Jasper raises his hands and laughs. "Margo is doing all this on her own. Only a queen can rule, and I don't want any such power. I've been a prisoner here as long as everyone else."

Before I can stop myself, "You can walk through walls, why haven't you left?" He gets a sad look on his face and shrugs. "I can go through these walls, but not through the metal doors. They stop all magic from leaving. Our sister's sick mind game. Letting us keep our magic, but knowing we can't use it on anything helpful." He looks down at the ground and kicks it. My shoulders slump and realize I really don't have time to second guess my newly found family. I nod to myself and my magic swirls in my chest in agreement.

"I have a plan."

TWENTY-FIVE

CAS

I pace back and forth like some kind of caged animal. Ten steps to the right. Stop. Turn around ten steps to the left. Stop. Repeat. "I know this is hard for you guys but-" Before Mac can even finish her sentence, I growl out at her. "You have no idea what it's like to miss your other half. We can't feel her Mac. She shut off the connection. She might as well ripped out our hearts." I bang my chest to make my point, but I know I'm taking my anger out on her, but I can't help it. Azzie didn't trust us enough to tell us her plan, so she went off without us like we weren't a team. As if we haven't felt like we failed her many times before she knew what she was doing. *When I get her back, I'm going to turn her pretty little ass bright red.*

Mac raises her hands and steps back, and I resume my pacing. After another few minutes there is a light knock on the door and it opens to Birdy and Michael standing in the doorway. Before I can even approach them, Knox is up and in Michael's face. "You knew. You knew, and you just let her think she had to go alone. We could have come up with a better plan. She doesn't even know half of what she can do and you sent her to be sacrificed to her bitch of a sister. That is your daughter!" He is huffing by the time he finishes his rant and

I look at the others with a cocked brow. *So maybe the asshole isn't so bad.* Michael slumps for a second before taking a deep breath, but it's not him who speaks up. It's Birdy.

"Boys, I know this is hard for you all." She raises her hand to silence the protest on our tongues. "We both understand how hard it is to be away from a mate. You all know that my Henry passed many, many years ago. Michael has been away from Queen Ava for eighteen years now and he knows she is a prisoner to Margo, so don't you boys dare tell us we don't understand." She looks over at each of us and we nod because she's right. I look over at Mac in apology. She might not have met her mate yet, but Azzie is one of her best friends and they have become extremely close. She nods in understanding, or maybe to just accept my unspoken words.

"Now, I foresaw what was going to play out in a vision. I made the choice to confide a few of the things I saw with young Azzie and Michael, and left the choice of action to her. This is her path, after all. She chose what she did for a reason, but sadly, I cannot see anything else that is to come. I understand that as her mates and chosen guard you feel the urge to go to her, but this is Azzie's plan and we must follow it for it to work. This will not be easy, gentlemen. We must arrive at the right time or Margo will win. So I need you all to keep your head and prepare for the battle ahead." She holds her head higher after that last statement, and my demon shifts under my skin.

"How will we know it's time to go to her?" Cain asks, and it's a good question. I never thought of that. Birdy looks over to Michael and then gets a sad look for a second before she masks it. *What was that about?*

"You will know." Is all she says before she nods and turns to leave. "I will make us all supper. You will all need your strength." Then she walks out towards the kitchen, leaving me with a bad feeling in the pit of my stomach that she doesn't want to tell us something. I look over to Michael, who stares after her but has a frown marring his face.

"Michael, what is she not telling us?" Max asks. We are all standing around the living room now. Caleb, Ivy and Mac all stay seated on the couch, but I'm sure the guys are just as frustrated as me right now with our mate.

He looks at all of us but stays quiet for a moment. As if trying to figure out if telling us will help or not. "Michael." He looks over at me again and I hold his gaze for a second before I continue. "We need to know everything. What are we walking into? How will we know it's time to go to her? Who will we be up against? These are things we need to know in order to protect Azzie. I know she is powerful and now with her magic unlocked and you training her all week, she is a force not to be messed with, but I have a feeling even she has limits. She doesn't know everything, and her magic is still so new to her." It's all the truth and he must realize it because he takes another deep breath and then takes a seat in the lounge chair to the right of the couch. He rubs a hand down his face and then looks up at us.

"I only know what Birdy saw. I also have my guesses of what Margo has planned and who may be present, but it's been many years since I have been home and things may have changed." He looks around at us and we nod in understanding. Any information at this point can only help us.

"Margo plans to have a grand affair. Since her takeover, she has held power since she was the last of the line. So, everyone believed. Recently, there have been rumors of the true queen still being alive. Of course, Margo has shut down those claims or simply killed those who try to say they should look for her. Margo still firmly believes that she can steal Azzie's power and make it her own. She would have the power to claim she is the new true queen by fate. Margo has only ever wanted power, and to flaunt it over everyone else. As far as we know, she is planning a big feast, where many of the well-known families will attend. She will also have Azzie and the rest of the royal family attend." Remi furrows his brows in confusion.

"Wouldn't everyone recognize the royal family? Surely they wouldn't allow Margo to continue on as queen if Queen Ava was found alive." Remi asks, and he has a good point but Michael just shakes his head with a frown.

"Much has changed since you boys have been home. Margo has always tired to rule by force and making it known she was the last of the royal bloodline, but when the rumors of the true queen possibly still being alive started up, Margo began to rule with fear. She is not afraid to end someone life to make a point."

"So you're saying even though queen Ava and Azzie are the rightful rulers, no one will go against Margo for them?" Kam asks, and Michael shakes his head again.

"So, who else will we need to worry about? What type of forces?" I ask. This is the most important thing we need to know. *Who do we have to destroy to get Azzie back?*

He looks over at Knox. "As far as I know she still works alongside your father but I believe he is only playing a part and once he sees you, he will pull back his men but the others that have followed her since day one will be the problem. I have no clue who or what we will face with them."

"I don't think that will be an issue." I smile as my demon puffs up under my chest, ready to find and protect our mate.

"You never told us when we will know it's time." Cain states again, and we all turn and focus on Michael again. He goes to open his mouth to answer when suddenly it feels like my chest is being sliced open. A deep burning pain sears through me and I groan out as I look at my hands to see if I've been injured. I see nothing and peer around the room at my brothers as they do the same.

Michael suddenly stands, knocking over the chair, looking at all of us in horror. Mac, Ivy, and Caleb stand next and look at each other in fear. Caleb steps to the side, then nods at Michael. "What is going on?" I grind out, sucking in a breath as the pain eases enough for my lung to expand.

"Azzie." Michael says in a hushed tone, almost too quiet for me to hear. He turns towards Caleb and nods back. "It's time." Caleb moves his arms and the lights appear as he focuses. The lightbulb finally goes off in my brain and I realize what this pain means.

The portal opens and I can see a grand ballroom on the other side with people already fighting each other, but the only thing I can see is her. I take in everything as she stands there in a deep red floor length ballgown. She is facing the portal, looking down at her hands placed on her chest, but looks up as if sensing us. Her eyes widen and she looks down again. From here, it looks like she is wearing some type of black pendant on her red dress in the center of her chest, but she pulls it away and drops it to the ground with a resounding clank and her hands drip with red liquid.

She looks back up at me and smiles softly, but the smile fades as she falls forward. Her knees hit the ground hard and then she falls to the side. I rush forward before I can even think. My mind set on only her.

What have you done, baby girl?

TWENTY-SIX

AZZIE

I finished explaining my plan to everyone after we made more introductions. I met my other dads through the bars of my mother's cell. It's still a little odd for me knowing I have multiple dads, but I guess I should get used to it. *I have six men just for myself.* My mom's men are all so different and not at all what I excepted but you can see the concern in their eyes for my mom and even me. Jasper explained that each of us have a different dad that gave us his DNA, but to him they were all his fathers.

His dad is Greg. Despite being locked up in this dungeon room for eighteen years, Greg still looks intimidating, with his green eyes, dark hair, and naturally tan skin. He looks kind of scary at first, but he also looks like a giant teddy bear with a soft smile that lights up his eyes.

Next was David, he is Margo's father, and when I stared at him, he seemed hesitant to meet my eyes. I figured it's because his spawn is the one who wants to kill me. He has dark brown hair with lighter shades that run through it that match his facial hair leading down and over his chin. When he finally glances up, I see his eyes are a bright blue color. He is built a bit smaller than Greg, but no less scary looking.

Last is James. His frame is leaner and taller than the others. Shaggy blonde hair with bright blue eyes shine with happiness but still seem shaded in pain.

My mother stays next to me the entire time I'm in her cell. It's almost like she knows I'm leaving out a part of my plan but continues to comfort me, knowing I need it right now. She tries to keep a small smile on her face as I explain what I know is to come. No one argues or tries to talk me out of anything, but I can tell they are all worried. I know Margo is more advanced with magic, but I have to trust my own magic and my men. *This is the only way I know how to save everyone.*

I'm about to ask them about their magic when we hear a door open down the hall again. My mother's eyes widen and she stands quickly, pulling me over to the wall that connects to my small cell. She nods to Jasper, and he grabs me by the shoulders and pushes me through the wall with a whispered, "I'm sorry" on his lips. I don't think I will ever get used to going through solid objects like its nothing. I finally get a full breath of air after a second of steadying myself and rush to my cot, just as I hear a key being inserted into my door.

"Well, hello, sweetheart. I see you're up now." The man from earlier purrs and I try not to grimace at the sound of his less than seductive voice, but I can't hold back the shiver of disgust that runs through my body as he steps into my prison. He is holding a tray with what I think is supposed to be food on it in one hand and a big black box with a red ribbon tied around it in the other. I luck out when he doesn't see my shiver and mistakes it for what it's not. He strides forward and I hear a bang on the metal bars as my mother tries to get this guy's attention. He rolls his eyes and places the box and tray next to me and turning towards the bars. "Calm down. I have orders not to touch, yet." He winks at me, then turns and heads back to the door. He continues to open doors and place trays and boxes in each of the cells. When he finishes, he raises his voice to speak to us all. "The boxes are gifts from her Majesty Margo. You would do well to accept the gift and be on your best behavior tomorrow for dinner. Your presence is required for the dinner and then a wonderful in-house show." He laughs as he finishes his statement and I hear him walk away finally. I roll my eyes at his phrasing of a wonderful show. None of us are stupid and all know what my wicked bitch of a sister has planned for me.

I take in my dinner and decide I'd rather not eat what looks like dog food. I've fed Grim and Reaper better food when they were hounds and I didn't realize what they truly were. A pang hits my chest as I think about my hellhounds and how they are probably freaking out right now. All my men must be pissed at me and I totally get why they would be. I told Mac, Ivy, and Caleb my plan before them, but I knew how they would react. They would try to protect me, hide me away and try to fight a battle that I must endure in order to save them. They can be mad all they want; I would do what I have to save my loved ones a hundred times over if that was asked of me. I lay down on my cot and cover myself with the thin sheet that laid at my feet. The black wrapped box falls to the ground, but I pay it no mind. I just close my eyes and think of my guys and how I hope they can one day forgive me.

I wake to a hand running down my cheek and soft humming noises sounding in my ears, but I don't freak out because the scent of jasmine and vanilla hits my nose as the person next to me shifts. My mother. Relaxing for a few minutes until the realization of the time dawns on me. I open my eyes and my mother smiles down at me and the sudden feeling of sadness washes over me. I have wanted a mother for years and hated that I didn't have one to love me, care for me, to protect me from monsters but while I was angry at this woman for not being there, she had to sit here with her daughter. To protect her family and me, she sacrificed her daughter and spent eighteen years living in captivity. She knew I would suffer growing up, but she also knew it would make me a stronger woman, but she didn't just lose a daughter. She lost being a mother to me as well. Missed all my firsts and seeing me grow. She also lost a second daughter to jealousy and rage, yet she sits here and smiles down at me with a knowing glimmer in her eyes.

She reaches up and wipes away a tear that escaped. She nods to the box, and that's when I notice she is already dressed in a beautiful emerald green dress that flows down to the ground and makes my already beautiful mother a shining star in a sea of darkness. I can see why my dad fell in love with her.

I sit up and grab the box, untying the red silk ribbon bow and opening the black box with caution. I suppose if she wanted to kill me already; she has had many chances. When I look down at its contents, my eyes go a little wide. In the box lies a stunning, deep silk red gown that feels amazing. It's soft and is the most beautiful thing I have ever seen.

My mother takes out the item and holds it up to me with a big grin. She nods to me and I change into the dress, a little stunned that it fits like a glove. I smooth my hand down the front of it and smile a little. It really is a gorgeous dress, and it's a shame that it's going to get ruined tonight. My mother runs her finger in a circle around my face and I frown at her until she holds up a small pocket mirror and I see that I have a light layer of natural looking makeup on my face. She added a shade of blood red on my lips that ties the look together perfectly and I once again wish I had this woman in my life growing up.

Sadly, our bonding moment ends too quickly when the door from down the hall is heard opening and multiple footsteps can stomp coming towards us. My mother glances at me once more, then rushes to her wall and steps through, much like Jasper did. *Whoa, maybe I can learn to do that too.* The man from yesterday opens my door and stands there with a pair of gold bracelets hanging around a finger and smirk on his face. "Now, let's do this the easy way, yeah?" I simply nod because I know there is no point in fighting this and I know this is not the right time. He steps forward and places the gold cuffs on my wrist and secures them. I look down at them and notice that they have a beautiful design on them, but I know these aren't just for looks. I cock a brow in question, and his smirk turns into a full-blown smile. "They made these special just for you, so you can't use any of your magic, sweetheart. We wouldn't want you to fight back now, would we?" I know it's a rhetorical question, so as much as I want to snark back, I hold my tongue. I peer back down at my new jewelry. My magic chooses that moment to shift deep in my chest, making me aware that these cuffs don't actually work on me. I figured they wouldn't since I'm not a normal queen of Hell, but I still don't understand what being the Chaos Queen means. I suppose I'll find out soon enough.

He grabs ahold of my upper arm and walks me out of the little cell into the hallway where I see my mother, Jasper, Greg, David and

James, all in fancy outfits and matching gold cuffs on them as well. A guard has a hold of each of them, much like mine does, and then they start walking us towards the door at the end. As we walk, I wonder if the others still have their magic, even with the cuff on or if it's just me.

We go through the door and head up a winding stone staircase till we hit another hallway. Hallway after hallway passes and I begin to wonder if we even have an end in sight until we come to two large wooden doors with unique symbols lining the frame. We stop for a minute and the guard up front holding my mother's arm knocks until the doors are being pulled open and I can hear a very familiar male voice introduce us as honored guests.

My mother straightens her spine and holds her head that much higher as she steps forward and gasps sound around the room. Jasper mirrors our mother's movement, and steps forward next. Greg, David and then James all following suit as the room seems frozen in shock. I suppose eighteen years of believing the royal family being dead and then suddenly dressed all fancy and showing up to a royal dinner party would be a shock to the system.

The asshole guard pulls me forward a bit but waits at the entrance as they escort my family to their seats. After they are secured in their places, a fresh voice raises and I know this one from my weird dream place. "Ladies and gentlemen, it is a great honor for you all to join me tonight to celebrate a day that will go down in our history books. For today is the day that I, as your rightful queen, have reunited the lost royal family. My mother, your former queen Ava, and her men, my fathers Greg, David, and James; even the young prince Jasper has joined us today for a truly glorious celebration." Murmurs go up around the room and Margo raises her hand, and the room goes silent once again. "I know you have many questions, but as your queen, I had to do what was right for our people. I knew that my mother was no longer fit to be the ruling queen and decided to remove her from power and take my rightful place are the true queen." She pauses and looks across the room as if waiting for someone to deny her claim. She nods to herself and then continues, "With that being said, the rumor of the young princess being the next true queen were true." More gasps can be heard, but no one moves a muscle. The tension in the room climbing. "Today is the young princesses eighteenth birthday and to celebrate she will be handing over her power and claim over the throne to me today as a gift." She smiles widely, showing off her white teeth. Like this is an everyday thing to threaten your younger sister and family. The asshole pushes me forward and I stumble, but catch myself before I can fall face first on the marbled floor.

"I give you young princess Azzie Morningstar." She claps like this is some exciting news and not some type of death march, but after a second the rest of the room joins in as I'm led to a seat right next to the wicked bitch.

Margo looks at me and her face fills with excitement. "Hello little sister."

TWENTY-SEVEN

AZZIE

I stare at Margo for a second, wondering what went wrong with her. *Why did she hate me when I was barely new to this world? Is it really because I bore a mark that I knew nothing of? Why did she have to turn my entire world upside down?* She ripped me away from my mother, my family, from a world that I should have grown up in, but now I'm struggling to get my footing and hoping I'm making the right choice today.

Birdy warned me that my efforts of today could change nothing and that the future is never truly written in stone and could change at any second. Deep down I knew she was right and that I should have come up with a Plan B through Z and figured out which had the best chance of success. A part of me just knows this must be done and I have to put faith in my men to follow through and trust I know what I'm doing.

"Margo, I presume?" I ask in a bored tone, but I already know. She sounds exactly as she did when I heard her in my visions of the past. She sneers over at me but quickly masks her reaction with a smile on black painted lips, fitting. I finally take a moment and look her over. She's beautiful, wearing a tight black gown that sparkles in the dim lighting. The dress flares out once it hits her hips and flows to the ground in soft waves. She takes after David with a pair of bright blue eyes and dark chocolate brown hair that flows straight down her back. Her make up is dark and heavy, giving her a dark, ruthless look. She waves her hand to the chair next to her in a dismissive move and looks to the room again as I take my seat.

"Now, since everyone has finally arrived, let's eat. After our meal, I have a big announcement to make." She takes her seat and claps her hands, as people pour out of a side door with plates and wine bottles in hand. They go around, setting plates down and pouring glasses of red and white wine throughout the room. When a man sets a plate in front of me, I see it's full of steak, seasoned fried potatoes, a small salad, and steamed veggies. My stomach rumbles, but I refuse to eat a single thing. I need to stay alert in case it was drugged or poisoned for what's next.

"Are you not hungry, little sister?" Margo asks sweetly, cutting a small piece of her steak and placing it in her mouth.

I smile back, "I'm afraid not." I reply when I really want to ask a million questions like, why did you do all this? Did you really hate me this much? Why did you treat your own family so badly? Why Frank? But I hold my tongue and continue to observe the room and see most of the guests staring at our end of the table with a wide range of emotions. Some seem confused, worried, even scared or nervous, while others seem almost giddy. Like they might be excited about the show to come. I know most of these guests must know Margo is not sane and that the show she spoke of is probably nothing good, but I can't help to think the guests with giddy looks must be my sisters' loyal followers.

Dinner continues on, with Margo eating her meal and the rest of her family watching her. She pays no mind that none of us has touched our food or drink or even responded to her and her many random small talk attempts. Once she finishes her meal and her second glass of wine, she stands and the room becomes quiet. She waits a minute to ramp up the suspense, I'm sure, but it must work since it seems everyone is waiting with bated breath and at the edge of their seats for her to continue.

"As you all may know, young Azzie here has the mark of the true queen, but today, we are all here to witness history. Today, a marked true queen will transfer her power over to the rightful queen. Me." You could hear a pin drop after Margo finishes her statement. I stand there with my spine stiff and my head held high as I peer over at the crowd. I refuse to cower to Margo, to anyone ever again. She is no different from any other bully I've come across, and I will not bow to her. *I am the rightful queen and it's about time she realized that.*

My magic shifts, wanting to come out and play, but it's not time to pull a power move, not yet at least. So, here's to hoping my guys are ready. I look over at my family and nod slightly. My mother's eyes widen for half a second before she masks her fear with determination. I think she knows what I'm about to do, but there is no other way to save them.

To save Hell. To save my family. To save my men.

"No." I say to the room and Margo tenses before slowly turning. "Excuse me." She says, dropping the sweet façade and showing her true self. I turn to face her fully so that my family can move into position. I knew that talking out and back at her would get everyone's attention on me and the drama about to unfold. Away from my mother and fathers moving around the room. They were hesitant about this plan at first, knowing I would be in the direct line of Margo's anger, but this needs to be done. Not everyone here is loyal to Margo and her wicked ways, and I won't allow those to suffer when all they have been doing is trying to survive under my sister's rule.

"I said no. I will transfer nothing to you." I repeat it in a calm, clear voice. She stares at me and then laughs. "Do you really think you can stop me? I have years of learned magic and you barely have a single ounce. You haven't even come into your powers yet. You will transfer your power to me or I will make sure your little mates suffer, all because you couldn't just bow to me like everyone else." She replies with venom lacing her words, but the moment she mentioned my mates, she crossed the line.

"You think no one knows you are the one who persuaded the Shadowland's to attack us? You think you can truly transfer my power to you with a simple spell? Not everyone is afraid of you, sister. You made sure I grew up weak, clueless, broken with a man who ensured I was afraid, but you didn't realize that while he may have scarred my body and made me afraid for a short time, he never truly broke me. He only made me stronger." I smirk at her and it must be that look and my outer lack of fear that makes her snap.

"How dare you think you can come in here and make a mockery of me? I am the rightful queen now and you are a mere stupid girl. You will bow to me. You will give me your power or I will rip it out of you." She screams at me and I continue to hold strong, my spine harden and gaze never faltering, which pisses her off more. She moves towards me, reaching for something on her side, and I know this is about to turn from bad to horrible.

I look behind her and meet eyes with my mother, she must see what Margo is holding because she steps forward, reaching for me, her mouth opening in a scream but before I can clearly see the object in Margo's hand she raises it and comes down in an arc towards my chest. I'm very conscious of the pain this will cause. I know I should actively avoid this blow. My body wanted to defend itself like we were taught, but I knew that this had to occur. I focus on my mother, as tears fall from her eyes and then the searing pain hits. It burns through me and at first I keep the pain from the guys, but my magic flickers and I let go of my hold. "Come to me." I whisper. Hoping I have just enough magic to call to them.

I look down at my chest and see a small black dagger with a gold handle sticking out of my chest. I reach for it, intending to remove it, but freeze when I feel the shift of air. When I glance up, I see a portal opening and my eyes meet Cas's dark ones. He's standing with his hand to his chest and stumbles forward, but pauses to take in the surrounding room.

The once quiet room is now in an all-out brawl. My fathers are each fighting one or two guards with my mother safely tucked behind them. She is flicking her wrist like when Caleb casts his magic and I wonder if she can still cast without her voice. Jasper is also holding his own as he fights two guys coming at him with blades, but in the blink of an eye, Jasper is now holding a sword of his own. It's then that I realize guests are fighting against other guests. I can see shifted forms and magic being thrown about as madness ensures. I was right that not everyone wanted to follow Margo so blindly.

When my eyes meet Cas's once again, my magic flares and tries to reach for my mates, knowing they can help, but I think I'm too late this time. I glance back down and grab the dagger by the handle and yank till it's out and blood begins to flow freely down my stomach and fingers. I released the dagger and feel a wave of dizziness, my head becoming light as I drop it to the ground with a resounding clunk. The blood on my hands is trickling down as I glance back at the entrance of the portal and give my men a gentle smile. At least I think I smile because the next thing I know, I'm falling. My knees hit the ground hard and then I'm crashing to the side. I can see Cas and my men rushing through the portal and Michael right behind them. He spots me, but his head wipes to the side and I know he senses my mother. I hope he goes to her. She needs him.

My vision blurs and I can feel the blanket of icy grip of the abyss start to cover me. Someone drops in front of me, but I can't tell who. They lift my head and place it in their lap and stroke the hair away from my face. Another person places their hands on my chest to try to stop the bleeding, but I know it won't help.

Blackness consumes me but before I go completely under I whisper to whoever will listen, "I'm sorry."

TWENTY-EIGHT

KAM

When the portal opened a minute ago, I didn't know what to really except. I knew we were heading home to Hell, but I wasn't ready to see the pure chaos of the room. I glance around quickly, taking in the room and see a few familiar faces, but before I can relish the excitement of seeing my family once more, my vision narrows to a single figure standing in a deep red gown and holding her chest. My angel. She looks over at us and smiles softly before my entire world starts to crash and burn. In what feels like slow motion, Azzie leans forward and lands on her knees before falling to the side with a soft thump. Before anyone can say a thing, I'm rushing forward, fighting Grim as he tries to force a shift to get to his mate.

I reach her in seconds and gently lift her hand and place it on my lap. I look her over and see blood flowing from her chest and a bolt of fear runs through my body. *What happened?* I look up and see my brothers surrounding Azzie with the same look of fear and horror on their faces. Azzie barely has her eyes open and the scent of her blood is making it hard for me to control Grim. He wants to destroy the room and everyone in it. I can feel his fury running through my veins and I'm shaking from my own fear and rage, as they battle to be my top emotion.

I look down and swipe the hair away from Azzie's face, surprised that I can be so gentle at a time like this. Cain is next to me holding pressure on her chest wound and I spot Cas hold some type of dagger in his hand just behind him. I know the others are here too, but my eyes refuse to leave Azzie's. She looks up at me and my heart stops. "I'm sorry." It's barely a whisper, but I hear it right before she closes her eyes. Time stops and everything around me fades away as I peer down at her for a long moment, not wanting to believe what just happened. *No. No, this can't be happening.* I snap my eyes to my brother, who is frozen, staring at his hands covered in blood, Azzie's blood, breathing hard but I see the sheer panic as his shift takes over and his skin ripples and turns the darken color of our hellhounds.

I look over to Cas who is now vibrating as his skin shifts from his normal smooth tan skin to a dull gray. He grows in rapid height as huge black horns spurt from his head. His shirt rips as his muscles grow and expand with his full demon shift. Our control freak leader may have just lost all control.

Knox kneels to my side, holding our girl's hand and shifting between his shadows and his normal self like his magic is becoming unstable and he can't stay in one form or the other. Shadow, man, shadow, man. His fists clench like he is trying to fight it, but it's a losing battle. The look in his eyes is scary as his eyes shift to the edge of the room, looking at something or someone, but I can't bring myself to look.

Remi eyes are glowing bright purple and where my once calm, laid-back brother stood now stands a man who looks ready to explode in rage. Purple and gold magic swirls around him in a whirlwind but his focus stays trained on Azzie's face; like he can't accept what we all know just happened.

Maxwell is tense and stands at the end of Azzie's feet, but he doesn't move. A tear falls from the corner of his eye and he wipes it around quickly, then snaps his gaze to mine. The look in his eyes is of pure agony, like he has nothing left to live for and that's a dangerous thing for a man to feel.

Suddenly, the noise from the room filters back in and I stand on shaky legs, hands fisted as my claws pierce my palms. I glance back down at my angel and imagine her to be sleeping or simply knocked unconscious, but I know. The moment she spoke those words, I knew they were her last. I knew her heart stopped beating then as well, just by the simple fact I felt my heart stop with hers. *I have nothing to live for if she isn't here.*

I hear a woman scream and I snap my head to a woman rushing over to us wearing a long, emerald green gown similar to Azzie's. She looks familiar but I can't place where from. I see three men rushing after her towards us, but Grim doesn't take the time to understand why she looks familiar to us. He shifts and growls at the four as they approach. The woman flicks her hands toward me and my whole-body tenses and locks up. My brothers notice my growl and surround Azzie's body.

The woman glares, but it's also soft in a way. Almost like she understands what we are doing, but is annoyed that we are preventing her from getting to the angel on the ground.

"Let us through." One of the men demands, stepping in front of the woman.

"Who the hell are you?" Demon Cas growls out. Lucky bastard can talk when shifted, unlike me and Cain, who can only growl in warning. Shadow smoke appears in front of us all, and I glance over toward Knox to see he is still where he was a second ago. Michael appears behind the shadow with his hands raised. "Let her pass Cas. Ava is Azzie's mother. She needs to get to her if you want any chance of saving her." Cas nods but doesn't move.

Ava? Holy shit. As in Queen Ava. She steps forward and flicks her wrist at me again, releasing me from my immobile state. She rushes to Azzie and places her hand on her chest, while tears fall from her eyes. Nothing happens. Michael and the three other men kneel next to her and reach for her chest as well. Growls go up from my brothers and me, but they all ignore us like we aren't even here.

I take another look around and see the fighting is still going up around us. It's impossible to tell whose side anyone is on, but as long as they steer clear of Azzie right now, they can continue on. "Whatever happens, you guys need to keep everyone clear. Protect your queen and mate at all costs. Find Margo. This all needs to end today." Michael barks out, but none of us move away. "Now." He says with more force and with one more longing look down at an unmoving Azzie, we all head towards the battle.

Ready to raise hell for our queen.

We all move through the room as one, heading toward the familiar faces we saw when we crossed the portal. Our parents are all spread out across the back, fighting off men in guard's uniforms. Well, that makes this a bit easier, but they are outnumbered three to one, and more men seem to pile into the room from a side door.

"This should be fun." I hear Remi say through our bond and see him crack his neck from side to side. *Dramatic much.*

"No one gets near Azzie. Do you understand?" Cas growls out and Grim nods our head.

Knox looks around the room and stops mid stride when he peers at a corner of the room. He tilts his head and then grins. "Care to share." Max says when he stops next to him.

"Margo thinks she can hide among shadows, but she can't hide from me. She seems to be watching all this like it's a game. I can show her how fun we can be." He says, and I can hear the eerie excitement in his voice.

"Leave her for last. If Queen Ava can really save Azzie, then she should be the one to deal with her. Can you keep her in the shadows until they finish what they need to do?" Max asks, and I just noticed he hasn't shifted yet, but that could be because his dragon is so big he didn't want to hurt Azzie in the process.

Knox nods and we continue on, taking out guard after guard that we come across. I see the relief in my mother's eyes when she sees me and Cain, but she continues to fight alongside my father.

We take out most of the guards when a warm tingling feeling brushes across my skin and I snap my head over to see Queen Ava and the four men are glowing and radiating power around their little circle they made to surround Azzie. That's when I feel it. Something tugging at me, a piece of my magic, of my soul, urging me to go to her.

A soft feminine voice fills my head. "Do you willingly give a piece of your soul to Azzie?" I snap my head down to Azzie's face. *Can she really save Azzie?*

"Yes." I say through my mind, hoping if she can talk to me, then she can hear me too. "This will hurt for a second." Right as she finishes that statement, my breath is knocked out of me as I clutch at my chest, where a burning sensation feels like I'm being ripped apart from the inside out. Just as quickly as it came, it vanishes and I'm left winded as I peer at my brothers, who seem to be feeling the same way.

I look over to see Azzie, excepting her to be up and smiling or something, anything, but now all I see is Queen Ava laid out next to her and sense no change in Azzie.

I hear another scream go up around the room like earlier, but this one sounds more like a child throwing a temper tantrum. Shadows seep from the corner to my right to reveal a very pissed off woman wearing a black sparkly dress and dark makeup, making her look almost like an emo prom queen, and then it hits me. Margo. Grim growls and Margo gazes across the room and smirks. *This can't be good.*

She waves her hands and a blast of magic sweeps across the room, freezing everyone in place. I can't even twitch my nose and I watch in horror as she turns her head and I know she is zeroing in on Azzie and the small group. A wicked look crosses her face before it falls and shock, then furious anger replaces it.

A second later, the voice of an angel hits my ears. "Come to me."

TWENTY-NINE

AZZIE

When I closed my eyes last, I thought the dark abyss was going to greet me again, but I was wrong. When I closed my eyes to the dark and opened them again, I was in a beautiful field full of brightly colored flowers I've never seen before. They smell light and sweet and I finally feel like I can relax a bit. The sun is warm and shines bright in the light blue sky, like it's trying to tell me I don't have to deal with the dark again.

I take a seat under an enormous tree in the middle of the field and lean back to relax further. When I glance down, I realize I'm barefoot and wear a soft yellow sundress, and for once my scars don't look ugly to me. I can see all the ones that run down my arms and legs and I get a sense of strength when I see them. I know I tell everyone that they don't bother me and that they made me who I am, but I still hated to see them. Today is different. They make me feel powerful.

I'm not sure how long I sit here when the familiar voice hits my ears, "This place is real, you know." I snap my head to my mother standing there in a gorgeous white sundress that sweeps the ground. As she seems to almost glide towards me, a soft and sweet smile grows on her lips. When she gets close enough, she leans down and wraps me up in her arms, holding me tightly. Jasmine and vanilla fills my nose and I inhale deeper, relaxing into the comfort it brings. Letting her presence calm me in a way I didn't know I needed. After a minute, she takes a seat next to me and holds my hand in hers. "You know you can't stay here."

I frown. "It's so peaceful here." I say and she nods in understanding but continues to peer out at our surroundings as if in deep thought. A moment of silence passes before she speaks again. "This place is not meant for you. You still have so much to do, and your men are so deeply lost without you." I look away from her.

I'm aware of what lies ahead of me and that I'm not able to stay here. Despite knowing this day would come, I'm not willing to let go yet. I don't want to fight and part of me doesn't even want to be the Chaos Queen. I haven't even lived my life and now I have to rule a realm. I know the saying life isn't fair, but can't the damn bitch give me a break?

"I was afraid when I was your age as well." She looks over at me with a small smile. "It's scary, stepping up and taking your place as queen, but you were born to rule. I wish you didn't have to go through all that you did, but can you stand here today and tell me you would change a thing?" She asks and I frown again, but before I let my mouth run, I actually stop and take a moment to think. *If none of this happened, would I have met my men?* I know we had a rough start and we are still learning about each other, but my soul wants to cry and scream out when I'm not near them. They complete me in a way I thought no one would.

"I suppose you're right." I reply at last and her smile turns into a smirk. "Margo will not change mother but I honestly believe she was never truly bad. At least I hope she wasn't. Jealousy can be a powerful thing, but I can't let her keep hurting a home I never even knew about. I can't keep letting her hurt my family." Her smirk fades, but she nods her head in understanding.

She understands that only one of us will walk away today and I can't let it be her. Regardless of what she has done, Margo is still her daughter. We sit there for a few more minutes before I feel warmth spread through my body and then I feel it. My men's souls calling out for me. I look at my mother and she smiles and reaches up to swipe a loose curl behind my ear. She nods to me and stands, reaching down for my hands. I place my hands in hers and she helps me up and then pulls me into a hug. "Lets go home, darling." Home.

I followed the urge of my soul and feel this gorgeous place start to evaporate around me, and then I remembered my mother telling me it was an actual place. I'll return to the peacefulness, but in person and with my mates. I shut my eyes and feel the warmth envelop me.

I gasp as I come too. My mother shifts from on top of me and my fathers help her up. I look over at her and see she looks weak and drained. I glance down at my chest and see that my red dress is ripped where I was stabbed, but there is no hole or injury. *Damn it, I liked this dress.*

I don't know what she did, but I know she did something, and so did my men. I look around to find them when fear laces my veins. Margo is standing in the corner, a sneer on her pretty face as she whirls her hands around and my men seem stunned, but that's not right. No one in the room is moving, almost like they are being forced to stay still. Margo steps forward and towards a demon Cas who is holding a dagger in his raised hand. Like he was frozen on his way to attack my sister.

She will not touch my men. Something snaps in me then and I rush to my feet, feeling a little uneasy at first, but that won't stop me. "Margo!" I yell and she snaps her gaze to mine and glares. *She could give Bella a run for her money.* The thought of Bella gives me an idea.

"You're supposed to be dead. I knew I couldn't transfer your powers, but I also knew you couldn't take my crown if you weren't alive to take the throne." She sneers and now that makes sense why she stabbed me so quickly. I smile at her, knowing it will piss her off by seeing my unafraid of her, but I need her away from them.

"Pity you failed. You should have just killed me when I was a baby." I laugh, but I don't find any of this funny. "Ahh. You don't know the transfer of power wouldn't work till recently, huh?" Power sweeps through the room like she is attempting to use it on me, but I don't move. The power running through my body is stronger, superior to hers, even with her years of knowledge in magic and me knowing nothing. I widen my smile and laugh so more. "Margo, that won't work on me." Her eyes widen slightly but she turns back to Cas and grabs the dagger from his hands and prepares to strike him but I simply tilt my head and watch as all my men are swept up in black and red shadows one second and then standing next to me the next. *Well, that's kind of cool.*

I hear the guys all let out relived sighs at being near me. *Same guys, same, but now is not the time.* Paying no attention to them right now, I send out my magic out over the entire room to portal or shadow the people who opposed Margo's troops to the other side of the room. I hear gasps and murmurs as I continue walking gracefully towards my sister, head held high and shoulders pulled back. I remember Michael would always tell me, "You are a queen, so act like it." I thought he was joking when he said it, but now it's fitting, as I tell myself just that.

You are a queen, Azzie. So act like the fierce bitch you are. So not his exact words, but it works..

I approach my sister head on and stare at her as she glares at me. "I knew mother had an affair with a filthy shadowland being and here you are. Disgusting. You shouldn't be able to rule the Royal Lands. Your blood is diluted with filth." She sneers again and I'm starting to think this is her typical look with how often she does it.

"I will not be the ruler of the Royal Lands." I start. "I am not queen of this Hell." I say next and she looks almost stunned by my words. When I reached out to her, she flinches, her eyes displaying the disdain she had spoken of earlier. "I'm not simply the Queen of Hell. I am the Chaos Queen and you will bow to me." She scoffs before she cries out and folds in half, curling in on herself as pain lances through every inch of her body.

"What the fuck did you just do?" She screams panting, but I simply stare at her and form the ball of magic I just took from her. Letting it spin in my hands for her to see the power I hold.

"You may not be able to steal or transfer magic, but I can. You do not deserve the magic that you choose to do harm with. So, you will live as I have for the last eighteen years. You are nothing more than human." I say and then twist my hand as her magic begins to fade and then disappears into thin air within the blink of an eye. She stumbles back, eyes as wide as saucers, and fear finally evident in her gaze. She shakes her head in disbelief, but what is done is done. I can't bear to end her life and see my mother sad. She has suffered just as much as I have the last few years and she has already watched one daughter try to kill the other. She doesn't need to experience it again.

Margo starts to swipe her hands as if desperately trying to conjure her magic, but it's no use. She has none left. I swivel my head to take in the sight of my men, standing in awe. *I think.* Striding towards them and waving my hand behind me, Margo was engulfed in a gale wind as a portal materialized at her back. She gets swept through as a scream leaves her lips, but I simply close the portal and pay it no mind. *I need my men.*

I glance over at my mother and fathers huddled around her and she has tears in her eyes but she nods. So do my fathers. Jasper comes up behind them and smiles as well. I nod back in understanding. Me understanding that they are saying thank you for not repaying the favor of slamming a dagger through her chest.

I stand in front of my men and smile up at them. "Let's fix this mess, shall we?" They all look at me funny, but they will find out in just a second. "Take hold of me." One by one, they each step forward and place a single hand on my body. I'm vibrating with all the power rushing through me and I need their help to put it to good use. When the last hand touches my skin, magic rushes through me and connects with theirs. It's like a live wire. They gasp and I even hear a soft moan, damn Remi. I focus on my intent and send a wave of power through the realm to restore the land as it should be. As Michael's stories once told.

Once done, my power seems to feel more stable and I can breathe properly for the first time in a while. This was how it was always meant to be. The feeling of finally being home washes over me and someone yells out, "All hail Queen Azzie!" And I smile to myself as a small rosy blush rushes to my cheeks. One by one, the room all bow or lower to one knee. I hold my head higher. My men all step in front of me and bow as one.

"All hail the Chaos Queen, Queen Azzie."

THIRTY

AZZIE

1 MONTH LATER

I stare at myself in the mirror, remembering how different every-thing was mere months ago. I tilt my head, trying to see the girl I used to be. The one that piece of shit Frank made me into. The weak and scared little girl, but I can't see her. It's almost like she never existed, but I know the truth. He made me into who I am today and if the coward ever came out from hiding and acted like a man, I would thank him before throwing him to the wolves. I grin at that thought before I hear a light knock on the door.

"Come in." I call and my mother's angelic face pops in. She looks me up and down before tears spring to her eyes. I rush to her and pull her into my arms, afraid for her. I turn to Michael, who stands behind her, but he's not freaking out at all. He just smiles down at me before nodding and walking to the couch in the living room. They have been inseparable since the night they reunited. Wherever my mother is, my father is usually right behind her, enormous hearts in his eyes and all.

"Mom, what's wrong? Why are you crying?" I ask, but she simply holds me tighter. But after a few minutes, she manages to calm herself enough to talk as she wipes her tear-stained cheek clean. "Its nothing darling." She pauses and I think she won't tell me anymore, but then she continues. "It's just, I was afraid I wouldn't get to see this day. I feared I wouldn't be able to save you, but you never needed me to save you. You needed your men." She smiles up at me and I blush and smile back at her. I don't tell her I was also afraid that they wouldn't get to me in time and that seeing me the way they did would break them, but they fought harder. *They were willing to give a piece of themselves to me.*

I knew that taking that knife in the chest was going to hurt and that there would be a chance that I couldn't be saved, but Margo had to think she won and I had to trust in Birdy's vision. She had told me the night Michael started training me, "A life to save the many and six to save the one." It clicked then. I would have to give my life to hopefully save everyone else and hope my six men could save me. It was scary not knowing how they would save me, but trusting they would. I knew when everything went down with Knox that the six of them touching me and reaching out to me somehow brought me back from the darkness, but I wasn't holding my breath that it would be that easy.

"I didn't think I would ever have you in my life either, but here you are." I say gently and help clean a bit of ruined makeup up.

"I am the one that allowed you to be taken. We weren't strong enough to keep you safe, and I had to sit here and hope fate would play out right. That you would find your way back." She sobs again and I can feel the sadness seeping off of her.

"You did what you had to do. I do not resent you for that. I'm happy that I finally found you. That I finally found a family. Let's not waste time in the past and the things we cannot change anymore. We must look forward and build our home back up to how my dad used to tell me it once was. Hell was once rolling hills and fields of beautiful flowers. Let's focus on uniting the people of the Chaos realm and ensuring this never happens again." I wipe another tear away and stood from where we had sunk to the marble floor. Reaching down a hand and pulling my mother to her feet and she gasps when she takes in her tear-streaked face. "Oh, dear." She rushes forward and fixes her makeup and hair, and I can't help but smile. I never thought I would have a loving mother or caring father or even fathers. I didn't think I would find love or even my own kind of family, but here I am.

I take a second and fix myself as well. Running my hand down a red and black ball gown, enjoying the feel of the soft silky material against my skin. My mother looks towards me suddenly and smiles widely. "Are you ready?" I take a deep breath and nod, wrapping my arm around hers and heading out of the bathroom and to the bedroom door.

I stand before the crowd, looking forward and holding my head higher as the other kings and queens, lords and ladies begin to fill the ballroom. It's surreal to think a month ago I had died on this floor and by the fate's will, my men saved me.

I look around at all the men and women joining me for this day. The sea of beautifully colored fabrics of gowns and properly made suits of the men fill the room. My mother and fathers stand up front with all of my men's family. My fathers hover over my mother and it warms my heart, knowing she is safe and loved by her own men.

I look up around at my men and notice their eyes are already on me, filled with a wide range of emotions. Happiness, excitement, lust, and I know my eyes shine right back with the same emotions. We made it. We survived my sister's terror and came out even stronger.

A few minutes pass and my mother steps forward and turns towards the crowd and a hush follows across the room. She nods. "Thank you all for joining us on this glorious day. A day that will go down in our history books for the better. Today we crown the rightful queen of not only Hell, but of this realm." She looks over her shoulder at me and slowly out stretches her hand, asking me to step forward. I keep my head held high as I step up to her and place my hand in hers. "Today Azzie Morningstar takes her place as the Chaos Queen." I set my gaze around the room as I take in my surrounding. It is unnerving that I'm a queen of a whole ass realm and I'm only eighteen. My mother finally turns to face me and I turn to her. She is beaming at me and I smile back.

"Do you, Azzie Morningstar, accept this position, this power and promise to always protect your realm and your people? To uphold this honor with pride and ensure you will always do what is best for your people? Will you rebuild this realm and strengthen it and ensure that your realm prospers from this day forward?" She projects her voice so that the room can hear the oath I must swear to.

"I will uphold this oath until the day I can no longer protect this realm. I will ensure this realm prospers and moves forward towards a bigger and brighter future. I give my life for this realm." I say in a firm tone as my mother leans forward and nods to someone behind me. "Kneel my dear." I do as she says and kneel on to both knees. I feel a presence come up behind me and something hovers above my head.

"Today we all join together to bless this day with a celebration. It is my honor to present to you, your new Chaos Queen." She calls out and then a round, heavy metal object is being placed on my head and my fate is officially sealed. "All hail Queen Azzie." My father yells out behind me. I raise to my feet and turn back to the audience as my men join my family in yelling out, "All hail Queen Azzie." The next chant is even louder as the room joins in. "All hail Queen Azzie." My cheeks are burning at this point and I want to hide behind one of my men, but I stay where I'm at. Looking out at my people. My home. My chaos.

I raise a single hand and the room goes quiet in an instant. "For my first decree as queen, I say we celebrate tonight as a united realm. Join me with food, drink, and dance, for tonight we have all made history." This time, excited cheers go up around me and I smile wider as everyone spreads out and partakes in celebrations.

Movement from the corner of my eyes has me turning to see my brother walking into the room and heading towards Michael. Leaning in, he says something that must piss off my father because he clinches his fist and then gives a tense nod. Suddenly both men turn to me, Jasper with a wicked grin and Michael's face mixes with anger and sadness. They cross the room to me and Jasper leans in to hug me. "Sorry I missed the crowning ceremony, sis, but I was out getting you a crowning day gift." I look at him suspiciously and then turn to my dad in question. He looks around for a second before taking a deep breath and looking me in the eye. "We found Frank. We have him in a cell." He practically growls Frank's name, and a rush of panic races through me before I can stop it. He couldn't hurt me if he tried, but I still spent years fearing this man. My emotions must have broadcasted among the bonds because suddenly I'm surrounded by my men.

"What is it, baby girl?" Cas growls, looking around the room like he was looking for a threat.

"Angel?" Kam asks, while wrapping an arm around my back and I immediately relax into his touch.

I can feel the rest of my men around me, just as concerned, but I wave them off after a second. "It's nothing, boys, but I have something you guys have wanted for a while." I tell them, a wicked grin stretching my lips with the idea. "Lets go visit a guest who came last." They all give me questioning and confused looks, but I remain silent and move towards the cells, humming a small tune to myself.

We make it down to the cells and my pace slows as I prepare myself to see the man that ruined my life with my sister. He didn't have to do all the things he did, and I want to know why. I want to know why he felt the need to hurt a child so badly. We reach the cell door that holds this monster, and I pause. "Why are we down here, sweetheart?" Max asks sweetly, placing his hand on my lower back.

Only one word is needed, but it still takes me a minute to answer my sweet protective dragon. "Frank." I whisper and growls fill the hall, echoing off the walls and sending delicious shivers down my back. I reach forward, but a hand stops me. "Are you sure, my queen?" Knox asks, but I nod once and open the door. It swings open and there, sitting on the bed waiting for us, is the man that almost destroyed me. He looks the same as always. Dark hair, average features, grimy clothes. He looks up at me and smiles, and my stomach turns in disgust. Peering at him now, I see him for what he truly is, a weak, miserable man who thought overpowering a small child made him more powerful.

"I knew you would come see me." He chuckles out and my men all step forward, but I hold up a hand. "Wait." They all pause and look over at me. "I have a question." I raise an eyebrow at them and they step back. *Good boys.*

I look Frank up and down and notice the man is nothing. I have a feeling he won't answer my question, but I need to ask anyway. "Why?" He crooks an eyebrow back at me in question. "Why did you try to break me? Why did you want me so weak?" He shrugs like he doesn't know or just doesn't care, but he does. I can see the hatred in his eyes. To my surprise, he answers.

"You were just a job. It paid good. But I never liked kids and never wanted one. You were so needy. Always needing clothes, food, shit for school and what not." He waves his hand in the air. "Punishing you was the only way I got a break from your whiny little ass. But as you grew, that ass started looking real good." I can hear the truth in his words as he licks his lips and gives me a once over and I feel the food I just ate a little while ago threatens to expel itself.

A threatening energy fills the room and I know my men are minutes away from killing him. I take a step back and give Frank a small smile. "Thank you. I will allow you to go for telling me the truth." His eyes widen at my statement. "Seriously?" He asks and I nod, stepping out of the room. "But I don't think my mates will be so lenient with you." My wicked grin is back as I look over at my mates. They are all basically foaming at the mouth with excitement. "Boys." They are all staring at me, waiting for the word.

"You better shower after you play with him. I'll be in bed waiting." I wink and go to turn away as Frank moves into a fighting position.

"Give him hell, boys."

CHAOS

THE LOST QUEEN DUET

QUEEN

N. OWENS

AFTERWORD

If you enjoyed the Kings and their Queen Azzie then stay tuned. Your learn more about how Azzie and her men are adjusting to their new life and change the Chaos Realm for the good in Jasper's story. Join Jasper on his journey to finding his own mates and learning to live outside a dungeon cell. Jasper's story is coming 2024.

Made in the USA
Middletown, DE
03 November 2023

41714222R00110